Call Me

Jane Claypool Miner

SCHOLASTIC INC.
New York Toronto London Auckland Sydney Tokyo

Cover photograph by Don Banks

ISBN 0-590-33766-1

12 11 10 9 8 7 6 5 4 3 2 1   12   4 5 6 7 8 9/8

Printed in the U.S.A.   06

Call Me

A Wildfire® Book

WILDFIRE TITLES FROM SCHOLASTIC

I'm Christy by Maud Johnson
Beautiful Girl by Elisabeth Ogilvie
Superflirt by Helen Cavanagh
Dreams Can Come True by Jane Claypool Miner
I've Got a Crush on You by Carol Stanley
An April Love Story by Caroline B. Cooney
Yours Truly, Love, Jaie by Ann Reit
The Summer of the Sky-Blue Bikini
   by Jill Ross Klevin
The Best of Friends by Jill Ross Klevin
Second Best by Helen Cavanagh
A Place for Me by Helen Cavanagh
Take Care of My Girl by Carol Stanley
Lisa by Arlene Hale
Secret Love by Barbara Steiner
Nancy & Nick by Caroline B. Cooney
Wildfire Doube Romance by Diane McClure Jones
Senior Class by Jane Claypool Miner
Cindy by Deborah Kent
Too Young to Know by Elisabeth Ogilvie
Junior Prom by Patricia Aks
Saturday Night Date by Maud Johnson
He Loves Me Not by Carolina Cooney
Good-bye, Pretty One by Lucille S. Warner
Just a Summer Girl by Helen Cavanagh
The Impossible Love by Arlene Hale
A Kiss for Tomorrow by Maud Johnson
Sing About Us by Winifred Madison
The Searching Heart by Barbara Steiner
Write Every Day by Janet Quin-Harkin
Christy's Choice by Maud Johnson
The Wrong Boy by Carol Stanley
Make a Wish by Nancy Smiler Levinson
The Boy for Me by Jane Claypool Miner
Class Ring by Josephine Wunsch
Phone Calls by Ann Reit
Just You and Me by Ann Martin
Homecoming Queen by Winifred Madison
Holly in Love by Carolina B. Cooney
Sring Love by Jennifer Sarasin
No Boys by McClure Jones
Blind Date by Priscilla Maynard
That Other Girl by Conrad Nowels
Little Lies by Audrey Johnson
Broken Dreams by Susan Mendonca
Love Games by Deborah Aydt

O*ne*

Michelle Karlsen raised up on her tiptoes, put her arms around Adam, and kissed him. As he bent down to return the kiss, he murmured, "You smell wonderful."

"Eau de Pumpkin." Michelle laughed and pulled away from him.

"You're beautiful." Adam then buried his face in her dark brown hair. Since Adam was exactly six feet and she was only five feet two, he had to tip his head to kiss her hair. Bending slightly more, his lips trailed down to her cheek and then to the back of her neck. Shivers went through Michelle as Adam whispered, "Let's stay home and neck."

Michelle laughed and drew away from him again. "You'd do anything to get out of going to a party." She raised one of her legs and held her foot forward as she asked, "Like my shoes? Genuine 1947 saddle oxfords."

Then she turned around to show him her costume. She was a little nervous because she knew she'd used more makeup than she usually did. Her blue eyes were highlighted with green eye shadow and her skin was touched with rosy blusher. The baggy orange sweater was an old one of her father's and she was wearing one of her mother's old skating skirts with bobby socks and the saddle shoes to complete her costume.

"Too much makeup," Adam protested.

"It's Halloween!"

"Anyway," Adam went on, ignoring the makeup controversy, "I've decided I want you to come to the airport with me. Charlotte's plane will probably be late and you don't really want to go to that party, do you?"

"Your mother's plane will be on time," Michelle answered. "Besides, I have to go with Susie. I promised."

"Susie's a big girl," Adam protested. "Just because she's your little sister, you forget she's growing up."

"And you're a big boy," Michelle said teasingly. Then she said, "It's her first real high school party and she's nervous."

"We can drop her off, go in for a minute, and then take off," Adam argued. "Later, we can pick her up. She'll barely miss us."

Michelle felt torn. She wanted to be with Adam and she knew that he was anxious about meeting his mother's plane. After a week in California, Charlotte would be bubbling with plans for the future and Adam

2

would stubbornly resist her enthusiasm. Adam had his own plans but his mother would ignore them. Yet, although she knew why Adam needed her with him, Michelle felt her loyalty was to her sister.

"I promised her," Michelle explained gently. "You'll be back at the party fast."

"She'll probably want to move to San Francisco," Adam said. The edge in his voice told Michelle that Adam was really dreading Charlotte's report on her trip to California. Once, reference to Charlotte's enthusiasm for big cities would have sent a sharp knife of fear through Michelle, but not now. She had long ago decided that his mother wouldn't really leave La Crosse, Wisconsin, at least not until Adam finished high school.

As long as Michelle could remember, Charlotte had talked of the great advantages of city living. Though she had a good job as an Administrative Assistant to the President at La Crosse College, she always talked as though she might move tomorrow. When Adam's father had died three years ago, Michelle had thought Charlotte would really make the change. Fear had been with her constantly that winter of their eighth grade year. But Charlotte had continued talking of her plans and they hadn't moved. Now Michelle was secure enough to say, "Your mother likes to dream, Adam. That's all."

She wasn't sure that her answer had been reassuring enough, but it was the best she had to offer. Before she could add to it, Susie swept into the room. Her round face was shining with excitement as she reached up to pat the intricate curly hairdo in place with one hand; she held on to her hoop skirt with the other hand while she attempted a curtsy.

"Do you think the beauty mark is too much?" Susie asked.

Without waiting for an answer, she turned and opened the closet door, bending down to pick up a paper bag. Her hoop skirts popped up in back, showing a mass of white net petticoats. Adam said, "You look like an upsidedown wedding cake."

Susie raised up, punched him in the arm, and handed him the paper bag all in one smooth motion. She said, "Open the bag."

Adam rubbed his arm in mock pain and warned, "If anyone asks you to dance, don't punch him. Boys don't like girls who can beat them up."

"Chauvinist," Susie said. "Open the bag."

Adam pulled out a horrible rubber mask. Holding it away from himself with his finger and thumb, he asked, "You don't really think I'm going to wear this?"

When Susie nodded her head, he looked toward Michelle.

Michelle said, "Well, maybe . . ."

"Nothing doing," Susie interrupted. "Just because you two have been going steady since kindergarten, doesn't mean Michelle will let you get away with no costume."

Michelle smiled at Adam encouragingly

and said, "You can wear it for a few minutes. It will be fun."

"Some fun," Adam grumbled, but he carried it to the car when they started out for the party.

Michelle sat in the front seat beside Adam while Susie sat in back, pushing down her hoop-skirted costume and worrying out loud about whether or not she would really be welcome at Charlie's party. Neither Michelle nor Adam paid much attention to Susie's fears; Susie liked melodrama.

Susie's a person who will always have drama in her life, Michelle thought to herself as she squeezed Adam's hand. *Adam and I are comfortable people.* The thought pleased Michelle and warmth flooded her as she turned to look at the handsome young man beside her. He *was* handsome, with a straight nose, soft brown eyes, and crisp curly hair. His mouth was full and when he grinned he was really striking. She smiled at him, knowing that he was too intent on his driving to notice. But that was all right. They had known each other long enough and were sure enough of each other not to need reassurance. It was enough to be beside him.

She could see the excitement in Susie's eyes shining in the overhead mirror. She knew that Susie was hoping she'd meet some special boy at the party, or that someone she'd known for a long time would notice her and would turn out to be that perfect person.

For Adam and her, tonight would be just another of Charlie's parties, but for Susie, it might be Cinderella's ball.

Through Susie's experiences, Michelle was becoming even more aware of how fortunate she and Adam were. They'd never really questioned their love for each other and had moved quietly from their childhood closeness into a new awareness of each other when they entered junior high. Now they were juniors and their love was stronger, surer each day. Neither of them had ever felt the need to date others; they'd been so happy and close to each other. Watching Susie was fun, but she wouldn't trade her own sure knowledge of Adam for her sister's eager expectations. *I'm not looking for anything*, Michelle thought. *I've got it all.*

The car pulled up in front of Charlie's house and Adam switched off the motor. He said, "Maybe I won't go in."

"Please," Michelle and Susie said simultaneously.

Adam sighed and opened his car door. When the sisters got out, he slipped an arm around each of them and walked them up the long, steep driveway toward Charlie's house. The Johnson house was large and impressive with its wide lawn and perfectly tailored hedges. The white wood was trimmed with dark red shutters, and lights shone from every room on the first floor, though the party was in the large room that covered most of the lower floor. Except for a small garage, the whole lower floor was one huge room. No one in La Crosse had a more perfect place for parties and Charlie gave more parties than anyone else in the high school.

"Are you sure it's okay?" Susie asked again.

"It will be a good party," Michelle assured her, pretending not to understand.

"It will be a dull party," Adam corrected. He didn't really like parties much and often pretended to dislike them even more.

"I mean, is it all right for me to be here?"

"I told you," Michelle answered. "He said, 'Bring the good-looking sister — the tall blonde.'" She was getting tired of reassuring Susie, knowing that her younger sister sometimes exaggerated her nervousness. Michelle knew that she and her sister were very different in every way and that just because she was calm and not outwardly emotional was no reason to expect Susie to be the same. She reminded herself that even though she and Adam had been to lots and lots of parties here, Susie never had. To Michelle, Charlie was just Charlie, but to Susie he was the older boy who lived in one of the biggest houses in La Crosse and gave parties that everyone in school talked about. She smiled at Susie and said, "You'll be the prettiest girl there."

"I won't go in unless Adam puts on his mask," Susie announced.

Adam started to complain but changed his mind and pulled on the horrible rubber mask that was supposed to be the Hunchback of Notre Dame. When it was in place, he

7

growled and pawed the ground. Then he took each sister's hand and pulled them up to the door, where he knocked loudly. Charlie opened the door and said, "Adam, you look great! What happened?"

Adam growled again, then asked, "Is that you, Charlie? I can't see a thing."

"It's got eyes." Michelle reached up to adjust the mask so that Adam could see, but the eyes were spaced too close together. She finally gave up, saying, "You'll only be wearing it a minute. I'll lead you."

They stepped inside the house, wincing for a moment at the loud music. Immediately, Adam said, "I've got to go. Mom's plane gets in at ten."

"It's only nine," Susie assured him. "Come around and see some people first. See if they can guess who you are."

Michelle and Susie led Adam over to the table where the food was and Michelle said, "Hi, Ted. Can you guess who this is?"

"Are you kidding?" Ted answered. "He never looked better."

"We'd better let Adam guess who they are," Susie said. "Everyone will know it's Adam because he's with us."

"They would know me anyway because of my beautiful body," Adam said, but the mask muffled his words. Michelle squeezed his hand and pulled him toward a group of kids. She asked, "Now this is a game, Adam. Who do you think these people are?" At the same time, she nodded to her friends and said, "You know my sister Susie."

Adam made a few guesses as to their identities and then pulled the mask off in exasperation. He said to Michelle, "I've really got to go. I'll be back in a couple of hours, okay?"

"Okay," Michelle said. Susie was busy talking to one of the boys she'd introduced her to, so Michelle said, "I'll walk out with you."

Hand in hand, they walked back to the car. Once there, Adam asked, "Sure you can't come with me?"

Michelle didn't answer, but she pulled his head down so she could kiss his cheek.

"Okay, Mitchy," Adam said as he swung his long legs into the car. "See you later. Have fun."

"Adam..."

"Yes?"

"Don't fight with your mother. No matter what she says, don't fight with her, okay?"

"Okay." Adam's hands gripped the wheel for a minute. He was obviously thinking of the running battles he had with Charlotte. She wanted him to be a lawyer and live in a big city. He was going to be a veterinarian and live in an even smaller town than La Crosse. Though both he and Charlotte knew that the ultimate decision was his, she kept attempting to change his mind.

Seeing the signs of worry on Adam's brow made Michelle feel tender toward him. She leaned over and kissed him lightly on the forehead. Then she said, "Your mother wants the best for you. It's just that she's so certain what the best is."

Adam nodded, started the motor, and drove away. Michelle stood for a moment in the cold Wisconsin air, breathing deeply and thinking of her future. She would get her teaching degree in agricultural science. By that time, Adam would be ready for veterinary school and she would be teaching. They would marry and she would help him with his school expenses as her mother had done for her father. After he was finished with veterinary school, she would quit teaching and they would have two children. Later, when the kids went to school, she would return to teaching in the community and help him at the office. It would be a good life — a life of love and honest work. They would have each other.

Smiling, Michelle returned to the party. She was gratified to see that Susie was obviously having fun. Her cheeks were flushed with excitement and she was talking to a different boy than the one Michelle had introduced her to. *Susie will be fine*, Michelle thought.

Knowing that she didn't have to worry about Susie freed Michelle, but she felt lost without Adam. For a few minutes, she stood in a corner and watched the scene. Charlie's large den was spacious enough for the thirty or forty kids who stood in small groups around the record player or the food table.

One couple was dancing and several others formed a circle around them. Michelle knew that others would soon work up the nerve to dance and if Adam had been there, she would have urged him to break the ice.

Two girls from honors English were sitting on a black leather sofa in the corner. She walked over, then sat on the oversized orange ottoman beside them. Michelle said, "Hi, Kitty. Hi, Bev. Your costumes are great."

Bev was wearing a bright yellow yarn wig and a short blue skirt. The large freckles on her face were painted with blunt eyebrow pencil. Kitty was wearing a chartreuse silk shawl with fringe and a long black dress. Her dark hair was pulled into a bun and she had artificial roses in her hair. Michelle was surprised that they were wearing such outstanding costumes since both girls were rather shy and not very social. In fact, she'd been surprised to see them there because neither of them went out much. It was nice of Charlie to invite them to the party, but Charlie did things like that.

Charlie was one of those people who didn't seem to feel he had to follow the rules all the time. Most kids would be too worried about what other people expected to invite girls who weren't part of any social group but Charlie wouldn't even think about that. Of course, Charlie wasn't exactly a part of any crowd himself. He always seemed just a little out of things. Sometimes it seemed to Michelle as though he tried too hard but other times it seemed as though he wasn't even aware of the ways in which he was different from the other boys.

And there were times when Michelle felt sorry for Charlie because she thought kids took advantage of him, eating and drinking in his house without giving much thought to him as a person.

Of course, it was kind of hard to take Charlie too seriously, because of his jokes. He had been the class clown in elementary school and in some ways, he still was suffering from that image. When you mentioned Charlie's name, someone would laugh even if nothing funny had been said. Charlie had specialized in corny jokes and little games like dropping frogs in the teacher's desk in junior high, but now his humor was more refined. Still, with his long, lean looks and his sandy blond hair, Charlie was hard to take seriously. He'd never gone out with a girl and he still made corny jokes on occasion.

She saw him across the room; he was carrying two bags of groceries and Michelle realized he must have just gone out to buy them. She excused herself and went across the room to Charlie, asking, "Can I help?"

Charlie nodded his head and motioned for her to open the door for him. She opened it and followed him up a short flight of stairs to a small kitchen. Once there, he dumped the groceries on the counter and said, "Welcome to Chef Charlie's private hideaway."

The kitchen was small and clearly only an

adjunct to the den. Michelle asked, "Is this really your kitchen?"

"It is," Charlie assured her. "Or at least, it's the kitchen I'm allowed to use." As he talked, he ripped apart the two paper bags and packages of lunch meat and loaves of bread fell onto the tiny counter top.

"You shouldn't have bought this," Michelle said. "There's plenty of food." The long table in the den had been laden with dips and salads when she'd passed it. While there weren't many sandwiches left, there had been plenty of other things to eat.

"I told Annie that thirty kids need one hundred and twenty sandwiches but she said fifty would be enough." Charlie ripped off the tops of three lunch meat packages and added, "Got to keep feeding them or you lose them."

Michelle wasn't sure whether he was kidding or not. With Charlie, you couldn't always be sure. Did he really think that kids only came to his parties for the food? But then, maybe there was some truth in that. Charlie was always sort of on the edges socially. He wasn't very good-looking and he was awfully tall. Michelle guessed he was at least six feet three because he was much taller than Adam, who was six feet. Kids liked Charlie but he didn't play sports and he wasn't particularly exceptional in any way. Of course, he was in honors English, but being good in schoolwork didn't guarantee popularity.

She said, "I'll help you make these."

"Thanks," he answered. "I've never made a sandwich in my life."

She laughed, assuming it was one of Charlie's jokes.

He said, "It's not funny. Annie, the housekeeper, won't let me in the kitchen."

Charlie's eyes were round and light blue and she couldn't read them at all. Not like Adam, whose deep brown eyes seemed to change colors with his moods. She could always tell when Adam was kidding but with Charlie, she wasn't sure. She asked, "You're kidding?"

"Nope. She says the kitchen is her territory."

"What do you do if you get hungry in the middle of the night?" Michelle asked.

"There are always sandwiches and cake and stuff in the refrigerator. I'm permitted to eat anything that's prepared, but I am not allowed to cook anything." Charlie was watching Michelle as she began putting mayonnaise on several slices of bread at once. He said, "You're not only beautiful, you're efficient."

She ignored the compliment and asked, "But what if you are dying for a peanut butter sandwich and there's only bologna in the refrigerator?"

Charlie shrugged. "Then I learn to love bologna. If I know in advance what I want, I can order it."

Suddenly, Michelle had a vision of how lonely Charlie's life must be. He lived in a nice house and had a housekeeper, it was true, but he must be alone a lot. His father traveled all over the country selling heavy machinery. All she knew about his mother was that she didn't live in La Crosse. As far as she knew, there were no brothers or sisters either. She said, "You should get a dog."

"A dog?"

"So you won't be lonely," Michelle explained. "I read about it in a magazine. People who are alone a lot need to touch something. They get dogs and they don't get lonely."

Charlie turned to her and said with a perfectly straight face, "I don't want a dog. I want a nice, beautiful girl like you."

Michelle laughed and said, "Come on, Charlie. If we don't get these sandwiches finished, all your guests will be gone."

"Do you think there's a chance?" he asked. "Then we would be alone."

Michelle was a little uncomfortable with Charlie's teasing. She had a feeling that he was partly serious and she certainly didn't want to encourage him. She said, "I wonder if Adam's mother is home yet."

"Ah, the fair damsel drops the gauntlet. She brings up the name of my rival, but I will not be dissuaded. I'll pursue the lovely lady to the ends of the earth." Charlie raised his arms, holding a knife in one hand that dripped mayonnaise and a slice of bread in the other. He said, "My fair lady, kiss me once, so that I may die a happy man."

He puckered up his lips and bent forward to kiss Michelle. She pushed him away and laughed, "Don't be silly, Charlie. Someone might come in and think you're serious."

"But I am serious, fair beauty." Charlie tried to put his arms around her.

"Stop it!" Michelle said. Her voice betrayed some of her uneasiness. "You're getting mayonnaise on my sweater."

Immediately, Charlie backed off. He looked ashamed as he said, "I'm sorry. I'll help you get it off." He put down the knife and went to the sink to get a paper towel. Wetting the end of the towel, he started toward her again.

But Michelle shook her head impatiently and said, "Give it to me. You'll just make it worse."

Charlie looked hurt and handed her the towel. When she saw how sad he looked, she said, "You told me yourself that you didn't know how to make sandwiches. So how would you know how to clean up mayonnaise?"

Charlie smiled and said, "You're right. As a kitchen helper, I need help."

They worked together on the sandwiches very quickly after that, exchanging only a few words. Michelle had the feeling that in some ways, she knew Charlie better and yet she didn't know him at all. Had he been serious about kissing her? But he knew she was Adam's girl. She decided he had just been clowning around.

When they carried the sandwiches into the den, Charlie immediately asked Bev to dance and Michelle joined Kitty in the corner. Kitty looked stiff and unhappy and Michelle thought with wry amusement that while Kitty probably wasn't choosing to sit alone, Michelle was, just because Adam wasn't here. She sat back down on the orange hassock and said, "It's a good party, isn't it?"

Kitty agreed that it was and when Bev rejoined them, the three girls talked about the costumes that others were wearing. They tried to decide which they liked best and to guess who Charlie would award the grand prize to. Michelle glanced at her watch several times as she talked to Bev and Kitty but the watch seemed slow. Finally, she checked the time against Bev's and was dismayed to learn that it was a quarter past eleven. Adam still wasn't back.

As she chatted with the two girls, Michelle watched her sister Susie laughing and dancing with a lot of different people. Susie's golden hair had tumbled down and her costume seemed more like a party dress than a ball gown but she was obviously having a wonderful time. Her laughter rang out over the noise of the party and sounded like a happy bell.

Michelle's heart raced as she heard Charlie say it was almost midnight. Where was Adam? He should be here by now. She started toward the telephone, telling herself she was being silly. Adam was probably driving to the party right now and calling him wouldn't do anything except upset Charlotte.

Before she could get very far, a tall boy with red hair grabbed her arm and said, "Hi, want to dance?"

Michelle started to refuse, then changed her mind. Maybe by the time the music stopped, Adam would be there. They danced together for what remained of one record and then the red-haired boy asked, "Having fun?"

"Sure," she answered. "I'm sorry, I don't know your name."

"No, but I know yours," he answered. "I just moved to town last week. I've seen you at school. You're Michelle . . ."

"Karlsen," she finished for him. She'd have to give Charlie some more brownie points. Not only had he invited the two girls from honors English, but also Susie and the new boy.

"Derek Petersen," the boy said. "I understand Susie is your sister. And she's younger?"

"That's right."

"Is one of you adopted?"

Michelle laughed. "Nope. My mom is Portuguese and my dad is Norwegian. She got the Norwegian genes. I got the Portuguese kind."

"You're both pretty," he said. "I couldn't make up my mind which one to go after. But I decided you're the prettiest."

Michelle stiffened. "You should try to make up your mind about people based on something besides looks. Anyway, I have a boyfriend."

"Where is he?" The red-haired boy was smiling at her skeptically.

"He's picking his mother up at the airport," Michelle replied. She looked at her watch. It was almost midnight. Fear raced through her body. Could Adam have had an accident?

She said, "I'm going to call him now."

Derek took her by the wrist. "Sit with me."

"I want to make the call," Michelle said. She didn't like having this boy she didn't even know touching her. And he was hurting her wrist. She thought he had been drinking a lot. She said, "Let me go."

"Come on," he said and tried to pull her down beside him once again.

Michelle felt a growing anger. Where was Adam? And what did you say to a character like this to make him let you go? She didn't have any experience with this kind of guy. Why had Charlie invited him anyway?

She turned toward him and said in a louder voice, "Let me go."

Behind her, she heard Charlie say, "Let her go."

Derek let her go and mumbled, "We were just talking. Nothing to get excited about."

"Get out," Charlie said.

Michelle turned to him and said quickly, "It was nothing, Charlie. Don't make it bigger than it was. Come with me while I make a call. I'm really worried about Adam."

She took Charlie's hand and walked with

him to the telephone. She was so confused that she couldn't identify all of the thoughts and emotions that were running around her head. She was worried about Adam — dreadfully worried. At the same time, she was grateful to Charlie for helping her. More than anything else, she felt silly to have let Derek's attention bother her.

She dialed his number and Adam answered. His voice was curt as he asked, "Mitchy, can you get someone to take you home?"

"What's wrong?" Michelle asked.

"Charlotte swears she's moving us to Los Angeles," Adam answered. "We've been arguing for hours. I can't shake her."

Michelle said, "Adam, I told you not to let her do it to you. You know your mother is always . . ."

"It's different this time," Adam's voice was dead. "This time she's got a job."

"Oh no!"

"Look Mitchy, try not to worry. I'll call you in the morning. O.K.?"

Michelle's voice was choked as she asked, "Do you think she's serious?"

"She's serious."

Just by the way he said it, she knew that Adam had already begun to give up hope. She said softly, "Don't give up, Adam. Don't give up." But he had already hung up the telephone.

Two

It was two weeks before Michelle accepted the fact that Charlotte was serious about the move. During those two weeks, she switched between anger at Charlotte for being so selfish and anger at Adam because he couldn't convince his mother to stay in La Crosse. She also tried to find various solutions, including having Adam move in with her family for the next year and a half. When both her parents and Charlotte said absolutely no to that suggestion, she said to Adam in desperation, "Well, maybe you could move in with Charlie Johnson."

"Charlie?" Adam was so sunk in gloom that he seemed not to understand much these days.

"I know he's lonely and he's got that big house," Michelle said. "You'd have to get along with the housekeeper but I guess you could get along with anyone. And you could spend a lot of time here."

Adam shook his head slowly. He said, "Mitchy, don't you see? They won't let us do it. Your folks and my mom all think it will be good for us to be apart."

"Do you think that's why she's moving?" Michelle asked. "Just to get you away from me?" She knew it was unreasonable but she was beginning to hate Charlotte. She'd refused to spend any time with Adam and his mother since they'd heard the news. She was afraid she would say or do something that would cause a lot of damage in the future — when she and Adam were married to each other.

"We could get married," Michelle said. "If we were married, they wouldn't be able to separate us."

"They'd have it annulled," Adam said. His face was drawn and there were dark circles under his eyes. Michelle realized that in some ways he was taking this harder than she was. Adam had never been one to talk much about his feelings. Though he was affectionate and quick to give compliments, he had a hard time saying what he felt — especially when it was bad. Adam was having a very hard time now, she realized. She reached up and traced the circles under his eyes with a gentle touch.

She thought she saw tears in his eyes. "You know I care. I love you, Mitchy. This won't be forever. Maybe I'll find some way to come back this summer."

It was November fifteenth. They would leave on December first. Summer was a million years away. At the thought of the long, cold Wisconsin winter that lay ahead of them, Michelle burst into tears. "It's a long time away," she said. "And you don't even know if you can come."

Adam sighed. Part of the reason Charlotte had given for moving to California was that her job included free tuition for him. When he'd said he would absolutely return to the University of Wisconsin for college, she'd replied he would have to get a job to pay for it. He and Charlotte had said many things to each other, some of them bitter, but he still loved his mother. Eventually, he was sure they would come to an agreement and in the meantime, he wanted to protect her from Michelle's anger. So he said, "I'll be back in June if I possibly can, Mitchy. You know that."

"I know I hate to let you go," Michelle replied honestly.

"You're not afraid I'll find someone else?" Adam asked.

Michelle stared at him. The possibility that he would meet other girls had never even occurred to her. She'd been so busy missing him and being angry about his leaving, that it had never even entered her mind that there could be other girls.

"I won't find anyone else," Adam assured her. "There will never be anyone like you, Michelle."

The very fact that he felt he had to reassure her made Michelle sob louder than ever before. Desperately, Adam said, "We'll write every day. We can talk on the telephone a lot. It won't be so bad, Mitchy, you'll see. Even if we can't touch each other, we'll be close."

He held her in his arms, stroking her hair and trying to comfort her until midnight, when she went into the house to go to bed.

But after a sleepless night, Adam was relieved to hear that Michelle's voice sounded cheerful on the telephone when he called her the next morning. "Hi," she said. "Do you think your mother will give you time off from packing to let you go on a picnic?"

"A picnic today?" Adam asked. He looked out the window once again. It was snowing.

"We could go down to the park. Do some skating and have a picnic lunch."

"Sure," Adam agreed. "I'll pick you up in half an hour."

The park was crowded with first-season skaters. They'd just filled the outdoor rink a week earlier and there were plenty of people that Adam and Michelle knew. But Michelle said, "Let's not talk to anyone. Let's try and be by ourselves as much as we can for this last two weeks. Let's try and enjoy every minute of the time we have left."

Adam smiled gratefully. "You've decided to accept the inevitable?"

Michelle nodded her head and slipped her arm through his. "If all we have is two weeks, then I'm not going to waste it crying. We'll try and jam a whole winter's worth of fun into the time we've got. That way, June won't seem so far away."

She slipped her arm through his and Adam's heart almost broke when he saw how beautiful she looked. There was a light dusting of ice on her eyelashes and some soft snow sparkling on top of her brown hair. He bent quickly and kissed her, then buried his face in the warmth of her neck as he said, "I love you, Michelle Karlsen. Don't you forget that."

Michelle laughed and pulled away from him. "None of that *mushy stuff*," she said. "I'll race you around the pond. The exercise will cool you off."

"Going to make me chase you?" Adam teased.

Michelle took off, skating as fast as she could. She turned her head and laughingly called, "The winner gets the brass ring."

Two weeks later, the day before he left town, Adam gave her a ring. It was a tiny gold ring with a single pearl in it. As he slipped it on her right hand, he said, "It's not an engagement ring. This is an engaged to be engaged ring."

"Oh Adam, it's beautiful," she said, as she held her hand up to admire the ring by the light of the streetlight in front of her house.

Michelle said, "I have something for you, too. I'll go in the house and get it."

"Tomorrow," Adam said.

"Tomorrow is our last day," Michelle said.

Her voice was thick but she tried to keep it light.

"We've had a great two weeks," Adam reminded her.

"Skating, dancing, driving around the countryside, movies, and holding hands in front of the television," Michelle said.

"Don't forget building snowmen."

"There wasn't enough snow," Michelle said and sniffled.

Adam's voice was thick as he held her close and said, "Mitchy, it will be like losing my right arm."

"Like bread without butter," Michelle said.

"Or hot dogs without mustard."

"Or peanut butter without jelly," she said in a laughing voice.

The next day, Michelle gave him a wallet with her picture in it. As she handed it to him, she said, "This is the place to put the money you save to come to Wisconsin next June. Or maybe you'd rather have a piggy bank?"

Adam's laughter caught in his throat. Was now the time to tell Michelle he might not be able to make it back to Wisconsin so soon? No, he thought. It would be better to break the news gently. Besides, he hadn't given up hope. There ought to be some way he could earn money and visit Michelle. Maybe he could get a part-time job as soon as they arrived. Somehow, he would find a way to work it out. At least, he hoped so.

"How do you feel about driving me and

Mom to the airport in Madison tomorrow?" he asked. "Charlotte wanted me to ask you."

Michelle shook her head in hasty refusal. Then she sighed and put her arms around him. "I guess the answer is yes. I can't imagine turning down another chance to be with you."

"And Mom," Adam reminded her.

"Charlotte and I have managed so far," Michelle said. "I guess we can keep on our best behavior a while longer. But I'll have a hard time pretending I'm not angry with her.

"I'll drive you to the airport. I can stay all night with my cousin in Madison and come home Monday morning. I'll miss school but my folks won't complain. They feel so sorry for me. They act like I've got a terminal illness and they're afraid to tell me. Every time I come around, they're whispering and when they see me, they stop."

"You have got a terminal illness — love."

Michelle nodded her head and said, "I'll love you forever, Adam."

"Me too."

"No, say it."

"I'll love you forever, Michelle."

Three

Charlotte was quiet on the three hour drive to the Madison airport. She sat in the back seat and pretended not to be listening as Adam and Michelle talked of the weather and schoolwork. Though Michelle was grateful to Charlotte for not chattering about how great Los Angeles was going to be, she wished there was something they could talk about that would fill up the great, empty silence that was growing inside her.

By the time they were in Madison, Michelle felt numb, as though she'd been given novocaine and it had spread to every part of her body. *It's like a toothache*, Michelle thought. *A great, big, horrible toothache.*

Neither she nor Adam ate much of the Mexican dinner that Charlotte insisted on buying them. After the tedious dinner they were early for the airplane and had to wait another forty-five minutes before Adam and Charlotte were ready to board. Michelle was so tense from holding back the tears, that she was actually glad when they called for Adam and Charlotte to board the plane.

Charlotte turned to her hesitantly, then opened her arms and hugged Michelle against her. Tears were running down the older woman's face as she said, "I'm sorry, dear, but I really believe things will work out for the best." She seemed to be waiting for Michelle to agree with her.

Michelle swallowed and said, "I know you do." Then she turned to Adam and hugged him briefly. He held her tightly for a moment and then he was gone. She stood and watched as he walked through the door that led to the airplane. At the doorway, he turned and raised his hand in a final farewell, then mouthed the words, "I love you."

She nodded her head and smiled and then he turned and went into the tunnel. Michelle stood for a while looking at the empty doorway, as though he might turn and run back to her. But she knew that Adam was gone — really gone. She ignored the tears that ran down her cheeks as she walked quietly to the window. The weather report had predicted snow. Perhaps it would begin before they were off the ground. Perhaps the plane wouldn't take off. Perhaps . . . perhaps . . .

Michelle watched their plane taxi out onto the runway and disappear around the corner of the terminal. A moment later, she saw the plane taking off and she knew she hated the plane almost as though it were alive and deliberately stealing Adam from her.

Michelle was still crying as she climbed in her car and started driving toward her cousin's house. Her tears were on the inside by the time she knocked on her cousin's door, but she knew her face must be red and swollen. She was sorry for that. It wasn't fair to her cousin Beatrice, a schoolteacher she usually saw only on Christmas and once or twice a year when she came to Madison with her mother to shop.

Beatrice made a great point of ignoring her tears. Obviously she had been briefed by Michelle's mother, because she said, "Your mother wants you to call home."

Michelle nodded and went to the telephone. It only rang once before her mother answered. "How are you?"

"Fine," Michelle answered.

"Did they get off all right?"

"Yes."

"Was Charlotte . . . did you and Charlotte get along all right?"

"Mom, everything was fine." At the concern in her mother's voice, Michelle felt herself begin to dissolve into tears again.

"I was wondering if you wanted Susie and me to take the bus in tomorrow morning. We could shop and have lunch. Then we could all ride home together tomorrow evening. Maybe Beatrice could get out of school early and we could have late lunch. It would be fun."

Michelle shook her head, though she knew her mother couldn't see her. Adam would be calling her tomorrow afternoon at three. If they came to Madison, she'd miss his call. But she didn't say that. Instead she said, "There's a snow-storm coming. I think it would be more fun some other day."

"We'd like to come tomorrow. It was Susie's idea."

Susie had offered to ride to Madison today but Michelle had refused her company, thinking it would be easier to handle if she were alone. Now she wished Susie were here with her.

"Susie has cheerleader practice tomorrow," Michelle said. Susie would be trying out for the junior varsity cheerleading squad in a week or two. "Besides," Michelle added, "I've got to start getting used to being alone sometime."

"All right dear," her mother said. "But if you change your mind, call. No matter how late it is."

Michelle yawned and looked at her watch. Was it only seven-thirty? How would she ever get through the night until it was time to go to sleep? Right now, she felt as though she could lie down and sleep for a month. She was exhausted.

Beatrice seemed to feel that the less she said, the better. She offered food and when Michelle refused it, she offered her a book, Scrabble, or television. Michelle chose television and the two of them watched comedies until nine-thirty. Then Michelle asked if it would be all right if she went to bed.

Beatrice stood up immediately and began making the living room couch into a bed.

"I've got papers to correct," Beatrice said. "I won't wake you in the morning. Just make sure the door is locked when you leave. There's eggs in the refrigerator and cereal on the shelf. Give my love to your folks." She bent to kiss Michelle lightly on the cheek and said, "I'm sorry, honey. I know it hurts to lose someone. But he'll come back."

Grateful that her cousin seemed to understand that her romance with Adam was not just a silly kid's thing, Michelle smiled at her cousin and said, "It isn't too long till June."

Beatrice nodded and said, "That's my girl. I've lived for June ever since I started teaching school. Believe me, it always gets here."

Michelle slept deeply. When she woke at eight, her first thoughts were of breakfast. She remembered she was hungry because neither she nor Adam had been able to eat much the night before. Her hunger disappeared, lost in a black fog of depression. She had a piece of toast and wrote a thank you note to Beatrice.

She started home at eight-thirty, wanting to be home in plenty of time for Adam's call. As she stepped out the door, she saw that it was snowing, and from the looks of the ground, it had been snowing for a while. The sidewalk was slippery and Michelle walked carefully to the car. She was a little nervous about driving on slippery streets. She'd been granted her license in June when she was sixteen, so she'd had little practice on winter streets. As she backed the car away from the curb, she remembered the advice her father had given her, "You can't get in much trouble if you just drive slowly. Even if you skid, you won't go far."

She was glad she'd started out early; it would give her plenty of time to get home. Pulling into the street, she drove slowly toward the intersection with the highway that would carry her home to La Crosse. It was a straight shot, with no sharp turns and no steep hills, so Michelle wasn't really worried, though the snow was falling faster now.

She turned on the heater, the radio, and the windshield wipers and settled into a comfortable thirty-five miles an hour. Until the snow let up, she would play it safe at that speed. Ordinarily, it was a three hour trip. Even if it took her an extra hour or two, she would be home in time for Adam's call at three.

There was something comforting about the warm car and the falling snow. Michelle felt as though she were wrapped in a soft blanket and the ache of losing Adam seemed to lift a bit. She could almost pretend that he was in La Crosse waiting for her. She let her mind drift back over the last two weeks when they'd been so happy together. The hum of the car, the click of the windshield wipers, and her thoughts lulled Michelle into a state of mind that, if not peaceful, was at least a relief from yesterday's pain.

In the background, she heard the car radio repeating the same weather reports and traveler's advisory warnings. The announcement caused her to slow down to twenty miles an hour when she took the turns on the road. When the advisory changed from snow to icy rain, Michelle was not surprised. She was thirty miles outside of Madison now and the driving was getting more difficult. Ice clogged the sides of the window, on either side of her wipers. She knew that slippery ice was the most difficult of all driving weather.

Gradually, her mood changed to total attention to the road in front of her. The ice was thicker on the windshield now and she had only a little space to see out of. What's more, the road felt funny beneath her. She was afraid to make even the slightest turns without slowing down to five miles an hour. She saw that there were several cars pulled off to the side of the road and she wondered if the drivers were too frightened to go on.

Michelle was totally alert and absolutely concentrated on her driving now. She was having a hard time seeing and wanted to pull off to the side of the road and scrape off her windshield. But she was afraid of not being able to get back on the road. Finally, on a long, straight stretch of the road, she pulled far to the right of the right-hand lane, but avoided the shoulder because she didn't know how deep the snow was there. All she needed was to sink into mud or snow and get stuck. It was a long way between towns on this highway, and in this weather, a lot of the service stations would be closed down.

Scraping the window with her ice scraper helped for a while and Michelle relaxed a bit. She saw a sign that said Richland Center and she knew she was halfway home. Glancing at her watch, she was dismayed to see that it was already twelve o'clock. So far, the trip had taken her twice as long! Michelle tried speeding up but the minute she got the car up to thirty-five miles an hour, she had to make a turn and had to slow down again.

Stopping only to scrape the windshield, Michelle made the next hour of the journey in a slow crawl. Finally, at one o'clock, she pulled into the parking lot of a small diner. She was hungry and tired and discouraged. Wrapping her muffler around her head and face, she left the car and dashed into the diner. The sharp wind hurt and the icy rain stabbed at her. Once inside, she was glad to breathe the warm air. Michelle ordered a cup of tea and a hamburger. While she waited for the burger, she decided she'd better call home. Her folks might be worried and since all the schools were closed, Susie and her mother would be home. Her mother worked half-time as a teacher's aide in kindergarten classes. The other half of the time, she worked in Michelle's father's electrical contracting business. Michelle glanced at her watch once again. It was one-thirty; they would probably all three be in the kitchen eating lunch. And if she knew her family, her mother would be worrying and her father would be telling her what a good driver Michelle was. She could almost hear her father's deep, humorous voice saying, "I know the kid can drive. I taught her myself."

Sure enough, Susie answered the telephone and quickly asked, "Are you all right?"

"I'm fine. I'm in Readstown and I'll be late. Didn't want Mom to worry."

"Here she is," Susie said. Michelle was pretty sure that the phone was being grabbed away from her sister.

"Where are you?" her mother demanded.

"In Readstown."

"Stay right there. We'll come after you."

"Mom, that's silly. Let me talk to Dad."

Her father's voice also sounded worried as he said, "Mitchy? How are the roads?"

"They're a bit slippery, Dad. But I'll be fine."

"We'll come after you," her father said. "Stay right where you are."

"Dad! I can drive home. I got this far all right."

"It will take us a while. Just sit tight." Her father's voice sounded really worried.

"I'm a good driver," Michelle said. "You taught me yourself. Have a little faith in your ability as a teacher."

There was a silence and she could hear her mother and father having a short, fast argument. While she strained to listen, the operator came on and told her that her three minutes were up. She promised to pay more money in just a minute, when she got change, but the operator cut her off.

For a moment, Michelle considered not calling them back. She would just keep driving and that way, they wouldn't have to come after her. But she knew that was a terrible thing to do to her parents so she called back, this time reversing the charges. Her father's voice sounded scared but calmer than before. He said, "Now listen to me, Mitchy, you've got a blanket and a first aid kit in the car. There are some flares in the trunk also. If anything happens to the car, send up a flare and sit inside the car in your blanket. I don't want you walking in this weather. All right?"

"All right." She did not bother to tell her father that if the snow was freezing into ice, it was fairly warm for a Wisconsin winter.

"And the main danger is skidding. So you have to promise me you won't drive over twenty miles an hour."

"I've been taking the turns even slower than that."

"On the turns, go five miles an hour. Promise."

"I promise. Don't worry about me and tell Mom not to worry. Okay?"

"We want you to call us again in about an hour."

Michelle looked at her watch. It was almost

two o'clock. Adam would be calling around three. She said, "Dad, I'm expecting a call from Adam. Will you tell him I'll call later and get the number of his motel?"

"Just be careful to drive slowly. We'll talk to Adam. You're precious to us, Shell."

Michelle hung up the telephone with a lump in her throat. Her father hadn't called her Shell since she was a tiny girl, so she knew he was really worried about her. But beyond that, she now accepted the fact that she would miss Adam's first telephone call. It hurt to realize how far away they really were.

She ate her hamburger slowly, knowing it no longer mattered that she was losing time. She drank a second cup of tea to fortify her for the cold outside. She thought about ordering a piece of pie but her appetite was gone, so she paid the check and left a tip. Then she put on her gloves and went out to the car again.

It was colder now and the icy snow hit her face as though it were a million sharp knives. Michelle ducked quickly into the car and turned on the motor. She tried to back out but discovered that her wheels were spinning on the slick, fresh ice. Carefully, she pulled forward, inching her way past the car next to her and pulling out onto the highway with the speed of a turtle.

Once on the highway, she breathed a sigh of relief. She knew there was less chance of getting stuck there than on the side streets or in the parking lots. As long as she drove slowly and stayed on the highway, she told herself, she would be fine.

Driving remained difficult; she got out to scrape the window twice in the next hour. At about three-fifteen, she called home again, saying she was almost there, although she wasn't sure how much longer it would take. She asked if Adam had called yet.

"Not yet," Susie replied. "But don't worry, I'll get his phone number for you."

It was almost five in the afternoon when Michelle pulled into the driveway of their house. Before she could climb out to open the garage door, her father, who was inside the garage, lifted it for her. She drove into the garage and she got out of the car and hugged her father. He kissed her on the forehead and said, "We were getting worried."

Michelle went into the kitchen through the garage. Pulling off her gloves and down jacket, she asked, "Did Adam call?"

"He called about fifteen minutes ago," her mother said. "We were so worried about you. Did Beatrice say she'd be out for Christmas Eve or just the day?"

"What did he say?"

"Who?"

"Adam." She was furious with her mother for not paying attention to her. What did she mean, "Who?" Who else would she be asking about?

"Susie talked to him," her mother answered. "But tell me about Beatrice. Did she say she'd heard from Jim?"

Michelle didn't answer her mother but went down the hallway to Susie's room. She opened the door and asked, "What did he say?"

"He said he wanted to take me to the dance, that's about all." Susie was sitting at her makeup table, brushing her long, blonde hair and piling it up on her head.

Michelle stared at her sister. What Susie was saying didn't make any sense. She asked, "Adam wants to take you to a dance?"

Susie laughed and shook her head. "No, of course not. I was talking about Tim Wilson. I thought Mom probably told you he's asked me to the Winter Formal. She was going to ask you if we could cut up your old formal. Mom thinks there's enough to make me a skirt and I can wear a fancy blouse. Okay?"

"What did Adam say?"

"Adam?" Susie frowned as though she was having a hard time remembering who Adam was. "He said he was going apartment hunting with his mother. Said he'd been to the beach earlier and had a sunburn. Said it was seventy-eight degrees today." Susie shivered. "Can you imagine living in a state where the sun always shines? I think I'd get bored. Don't you?"

"Did he leave a number?"

"Yes, but he said he might not be home. They were going to look at several places. He said it might be better if he called you. Can I, Michelle?"

"Can you what?"

"Cut up your old formal? You don't think you'll want to wear it again? You said you never liked it."

"Adam never liked the color. You can have it. Where's the number?" Michelle said. She had a hard time keeping the impatience out of her voice. Usually, Susie was less self-centered. But today she was impossible. Maybe it was because she'd been asked to her first formal dance.

"But now that Adam's gone, you'll be going out with other boys," Susie asked. "Are you sure you don't want to wear it again?"

"I won't go out with anyone but Adam," Michelle said firmly.

"Even if he's gone for two whole years?" Susie asked in a voice that was mixed curiosity and admiration.

"It doesn't matter how long," Michelle said. "I'll wait for Adam."

"Is that what you two decided?" Susie asked. "He's not going to date anyone else either?"

Michelle felt a little tight ball of fear in her stomach at Susie's questions. They hadn't actually decided that they wouldn't date anyone else, had they? They'd talked about their future together in college, but they'd sort of skipped over high school. Would Adam want to date other girls?

Four

They talked nearly every night for the first two weeks. Their phone calls were quick, unsatisfactory, and often left Michelle feeling she wished she'd said something that she hadn't. If Adam felt the same lack, he didn't say so. As a rule, he told her what they were doing and how the apartment hunting was coming. Usually, he closed his end of the conversation by telling her he loved her.

But hearing she was loved on the telephone wasn't the same thing as being held and hearing it. Each time the conversation seemed a bit more distant, a bit more remote. There was something else that troubled her; Adam's life seemed to be full of activity and change. Each day, he had a new adventure to relate, while her life seemed to be just the same. She told him some of the gossip from school, told him she missed him, and that was all there was to say.

After two weeks, her mother and father called her into the kitchen and asked her to sit down, for "a serious talk," as her mother put it.

Her father had the telephone bill in front of him and he cleared his throat as he said, "Now this is just the first four days, you understand, but your mother and I think we have a problem."

"I'll pay for the phone calls," Michelle said quickly.

"Darling, the first four days came to thirty dollars. Your allowance won't cover that," her mother said gently.

Panic attacked Michelle. What if they were to forbid her to call Adam? "I'll pay for the calls," she said. "Besides, after they find an apartment, we can share the calls. Right now, it costs too much to go through the motel switchboard."

Her father nodded and cleared his throat again. "We know you and Adam are very close. Naturally, we expected that it would take a little time before you adjusted to his leaving. But your mother tells me you've been talking to him every night."

Michelle said nothing. Without Adam's voice, she would be so alone. How could she bear it?

"We understand that you've decided not to date anyone else either," her mother said gently. "We want you to know we don't approve of that decision."

"You're entirely too young...," her father began, but he was stopped by his wife's hand on his arm.

"I'll pay for the calls," Michelle repeated. "I'll get more baby-sitting jobs."

"We don't want to be unreasonable," her mother said. "We love Adam, too. It isn't that we want to destroy your relationship with him. . . ."

No, Michelle thought. *In all fairness, my folks have always liked Adam. It's Charlotte who always thought Adam should date other girls.* As she thought of Charlotte, her fear grew. What was Charlotte saying to Adam these days? She was afraid to imagine.

"We just want you to be reasonable," her father said. "We think you could call him once a week. Talk, say, five or ten minutes. That would be reasonable, wouldn't it?"

"I'll pay for the calls," Michelle repeated.

"Michelle," her mother said in a firm voice. "You can't even afford to pay for the ones you've made. Your father and I have decided we'll split the cost of these first ones with you. After that, anything over ten minutes once a week is disobedience."

Michelle recoiled from the word, "disobedience," as though she had been slapped. Her mother never talked to her or Susie like that. Neither did her father. She knew that other kids had all kinds of arguments and friction with their parents, but it was not her family's way. Reluctant to continue the controversy, and knowing it was useless to argue with them today, she said, "You two have already decided, so I guess that's it."

Her mother nodded her head. "We're not asking for your agreement at this time. We know that you're very unhappy right now. So, we've taken it on ourselves to set what we think are sensible limits. You can always write to Adam, you know."

Michelle nodded her head. The tears were coming again and she was beginning to hate them. She had never been very emotional, but these last two weeks, it seemed as though that was all she'd done — cry. She asked, "If I earn the money, can I make more calls?"

Her parents looked at each other for a moment and by their hesitation, Michelle knew that they were concerned about more than the money. They were like Charlotte; they wanted to break Adam and her up! Knowing this made it easier to keep the tears back. She would show them all — Charlotte, her parents, and anyone else who thought that just because they were two thousand miles apart, their love for each other would fade. As she waited for the answer, Michelle twisted the small gold ring on her right hand. What would her folks think if they knew he'd said it was an "engaged-to-be-engaged" ring?

"We don't want to be unreasonable," her mother repeated. "Once you've paid off your half of these bills, if you can earn the money, you can make as many calls as you can afford."

Michelle's head was already spinning with ways to make money. She could baby-sit and she might be able to find a part-time job in a store. Working would keep her busy and help pass the time between now and June. She would save her Christmas money too, and that would help. Usually her grandmother sent her a check. Sometimes Beatrice gave checks instead of gifts.

"Christmas will be here in a week," her mother said. "I hope that you won't let your dampened spirits dampen the holidays for everyone else."

Michelle blushed. She supposed her mood had affected the whole family. They still were treating her as though she were an invalid, recovering from some dreadful disease. *But*, Michelle thought, *they expect me to recover. And now Mom is telling me to recover in time for Christmas*! She managed to say, "I'll try. May I go now?"

"We just want what's best for you, Mitchy," her father said. "You'll see. You'll get over this. You'll fall for some other guy."

But Michelle didn't wait to hear any more. She ran to her room where she slammed the door and threw herself on the bed to cry. None of them seemed to want to understand that what was between Adam and her wasn't puppy love. It was real!

She stayed in her room until suppertime

and then she rose from her bed, wiped her red eyes with a damp cloth, brushed her hair back into a ponytail and went to the table. No one said anything about the earlier conversation. No one commented on her red eyes.

Susie was very excited about going to the Winter Formal the next night, and she was bubbling over with questions for Michelle. Michelle answered in nods or one or two words, trying to ignore the pain and loneliness she was feeling. She didn't want to spoil things for Susie but it hurt so much to know that she would be staying home.

Her sister's happiness brought back memories of the last two years when she'd gone to the dance with Adam. The first year, she'd worn the honey-colored dress that would be Susie's skirt this year. They'd had a wonderful time at that, their first formal dance. Adam had brought her yellow roses and she'd worn them in her hair.

"Michelle," her mother said. There was exasperation in her voice. "Answer your sister."

"I'm sorry," Michelle mumbled.

"It's O.K.," Susie said quickly. "I was just wondering. Anyway, I'll find out all about it tomorrow."

Michelle didn't even know what the question was that she'd been asked. She was so busy listening for the telephone to ring and thinking about the past. She toyed with the food on her plate and tried to think of something cheerful to say. Her mother wanted

her to cheer up for Christmas and it was
almost here. She'd bought Adam a bright blue
sweater. Would it be too warm for California? She wasn't sure. She'd looked Los
Angeles up in the encyclopedias at school
and tried to learn as much as she could about
it. Knowing a little bit about where he was
might help her feel closer to Adam. Would
he call tonight? She'd have to tell him about
the new rules about the telephone.

The phone rang then and Michelle jumped
up from the table. She ignored her father's
voice in the background complaining, "She's
not eating a thing these days. She'll get sick."

"Hello?"

"Michelle?"

Her heart sank. It wasn't Adam's voice.

"Charlie Johnson here."

It took Michelle a minute to recover from
the disappointment, but she tried to make her
voice sound friendly. After all, Charlie was
not to blame for her miseries.

He talked about several subjects — their
holiday plans, the weather, and the basketball team. Finally, he mentioned the homework assignment in English. Michelle asked,
"Is that why you called? You want the
assignment?"

"I know the assignment. Read pages 108
through 156."

"Did you want help with the essay?" She
wanted Charlie to hang up. What if Adam
called and the line was busy? He'd call back,

of course, but what if Charlotte wanted him to look at apartments again tonight?

"I called to ask you to go out with me New Year's Eve," Charlie said. His voice sounded almost angry.

"Oh, Charlie, I can't."

"It's early. You can't have another date."

"I'm not dating anyone but Adam," she explained. It seemed to her that people should know that.

"Adam's coming back?" Charlie asked.

"No. I mean, I'm not going to be dating while he's gone."

There was a long silence while Charlie apparently thought this over. Then he said, "Well, how about if I have a party and you and your sister come to it?"

"I don't know. . . ." Michelle didn't know how to turn him down any more definitely without hurting his feelings. Then she remembered the time he'd tried to get her to kiss him in his kitchen. She'd thought he was joking, but maybe he'd been serious. Did Charlie really have a crush on her? The idea sort of amused her. Charlie Johnson wasn't exactly a fellow that a girl could take too seriously.

"Will you?" Charlie demanded.

"Will I what?" Again, she'd forgotten what the question was.

"Come to my New Year's Eve party. You can bring Susie for a chaperone."

"I can't, but I'll ask Susie if she wants to go."

"No deal, without you there's no party. You're my New Year's resolution, you know."

"I've got to hang up now, Charlie. We're eating dinner."

"How about the party?" Charlie asked. "Will you be there?"

"Oh, okay, Charlie," Michelle answered. She wasn't sure why she answered yes, except it would take too long to explain a no answer to him.

She went back to the dinner table and tried to eat a few more bites of her roast beef to forestall her father's nagging. The meat stuck in her throat and she was grateful when Susie cleared the table and brought in the dessert. It was a fresh fruit cup and much easier to eat. No one asked her who had been on the telephone and she didn't volunteer. It wasn't really important enough to talk about.

Adam didn't call that night or the one after. On the third day, Michelle was determined to disobey her parents' orders but he called first. His first words were, "We've got an apartment. It's in Santa Monica. Almost right on the beach."

Knowing that Adam was really settled into an apartment made his move seem even more real than before. She managed to say, "That's nice," and listen to his description of the apartment, but her heart wasn't in it.

He sounded pretty excited about the fact that the apartment was on the beach. When he said, "I might try and learn to surf," Michelle felt like crying.

"You'll be in Wisconsin this summer," she reminded him.

"Sure," he said. There was something wrong with the way he said it.

"Adam," she asked, "You are coming back this summer, aren't you?"

"I'm going to try my hardest," Adam said. "Mitchy, I can't talk much longer. Charlotte's keeping track of my phone bills and I'll have to pay for them from my own money."

"She's making you pay for all the calls?" Michelle asked. She realized her folks had been more fair with her than his mother was with him. She said, "I don't think that's right. She drags you all the way to California and then is too stingy to pay for your phone calls."

"My mother thinks she's doing the right thing," Adam said. There was that tight, controlled tone that Michelle knew meant she should be careful what she said about Charlotte. Adam could be very protective of his mother, especially since his father died. She knew it was silly to be jealous of the way he felt about his mother, but she was.

Michelle said, "Well, my folks will let me call you once a week for ten minutes on their bill. So we'd better decide on a time for our next call. I'd hate to waste any of the call by getting Charlotte."

"You could wish her Merry Christmas," Adam teased.

Michelle relaxed. At least Adam wasn't really mad about what she'd said about his mother. It felt good to hear his light, teasing voice again. There had been too much gloom in their conversations. "You wish her Merry Christmas for me," she said. "Shall I call you Christmas Eve?"

"Better not. We're invited to a party at my Mom's boss's house."

"Christmas Day?"

"Sure." There was a slight hesitation in his voice and then he said, "Call me early, O.K.? We're going to someone else's house for brunch. Then we're going to drive down to San Diego to see a friend of my mother's from college. I won't be back until three days later."

"Sounds like a busy schedule." She tried to keep her voice from betraying the hurt and jealousy she was feeling. Didn't Adam miss her at all?

As though in answer to her thoughts, he said, "I miss you a lot, Mitchy. I have conversations with you when you aren't there. It's weird."

"I wish I were there." All the old sweetness and love returned to warm Michelle. She was smiling into the phone.

"I've got to hang up now. Any big news?"

"None, except Susie had a great time at the Winter Formal and Charlie Johnson asked me out."

"Charlie?" Adam laughed. "You're kidding."

"When I said no, he asked me to a party New Year's Eve."

"That's more like the Charlie I know. I'm surprised he had the nerve to ask out a beautiful girl like you."

Somehow, his amusement at Charlie's invitation annoyed her. She said, "Charlie's a nice person."

"And I should be jealous?" Adam asked. His voice was still laughing.

"I'm probably going to his party on New Year's," Michelle said.

"Well, sure, why not?"

She wished she could see Adam right now. His voice didn't seem the least bit worried or unhappy about her announcement. But how could she really be sure what his reaction was unless he was there beside her? She said sadly, "I miss you so much."

"Me too," Adam said softly. But then his tone was businesslike as he said, "I've got to hang up. Every minute is costing me and I've got to save money for school and for Wisconsin."

"Forever," Michelle reminded him.

"Forever."

F^{ive}

Christmas came with a mixture of snow-storms, ribbons, and festive food. Michelle worked in the kitchen a lot, helping to bake cookies and pies and wrapping the last of the packages to go under the tree. She smiled at the pink and red striped paper and tugged at the brown satin bow.

But everything she did reminded her of other years when Adam had been with her. Though she smiled a lot, the smile felt as though it was pasted on. On Christmas Eve, her folks had friends in before church for a small celebration, and Michelle made it a point of honor not to mention Adam once to anyone. But he was with her in her thoughts and the past was stronger than the present.

Even the gifts brought memories of Adam with them. Susie's new skates reminded her that she and Adam had bought each other skates two years ago. The soft blue blouse her Aunt Meg sent her was just the color of the sweater she'd sent Adam. His own present to her brought tears to her eyes once again, when she opened it under the Christmas tree on Christmas morning. It was an album of love songs from around the world. With it was a note saying he was sorry he hadn't spent more but he was saving for the summer trip.

Beneath her blurred eyes, she could see her mother and father throwing worried looks at each other. Quickly, she brushed away the tears and said, "Let's open something else now."

Her father unwrapped his present from Michelle and Susie. They'd pooled their money to buy him a new fishing rod and reel. Though he protested it was too extravagant a gift, his face lit up with pleasure. During the rest of the package unwrapping, he kept the rod and reel stretched across his lap. Every second or two, he would run his fingers across the thin, shiny rod or touch the levers on the reel. He thanked Michelle and Susie so often that they made a joke of it.

"We're going to buy you a fish next year," Michelle assured him.

"Wait till you see the ones I catch with this. We'll have to buy a new freezer just to hold them," he promised.

There was a new coat for her and in the pocket was a healthy check from her folks. She could apply it to the phone bill, when it came. There was twenty-five dollars from Beatrice as well. Michelle began to feel a little more comfortable about money. With baby-sitting jobs, things would work out. She couldn't talk to Adam every day, of course. But she would be able to talk to him twice a week and she could write in between. She really didn't like writing, though, because by the time the letter got there, she'd usually already told him the same news on the telephone.

On Christmas Day, after the big meal, her parents wanted to go skating. Susie went along but Michelle chose to stay at home and listen to her new album. She sat on the floor beside the phonograph and listened to the songs about love. Then she began to play the album a second time and got out the new stationery that Susie had given her for Christmas. She began, "Dear Adam, Christmas just wasn't Christmas without you." Then she told him some of what had happened. When she'd covered two pages, she stopped and hugged the letter to her chest. What had Adam's Christmas been like?

She'd talked to him that morning, of course. He said the Christmas Eve party was boring but maybe he just said that to make her feel better. Maybe it wasn't boring at all. And now he was driving down to San Diego with Charlotte. They would have dinner in a restaurant on the beach. Probably fish, Adam had said. What kind of Christmas could it be if you ate fish? Michelle drifted into a daydream in which Adam was telling her how much he loved Wisconsin winters.

When Susie and her folks came in from their skating, they found her asleep on the floor between the fireplace and the phonograph. She woke to hear her father's voice saying to his wife, "That's it. You've got to do something about this."

"Give her time, Ned."

"She's getting thin. She's miserable all the time."

"What do you want me to do?" her mother asked. Michelle carefully kept her eyes closed to avoid another confrontation.

"Get her another boyfriend!" her father barked.

Even when Susie and her mother broke into laughter, he didn't seem to understand what was funny. "Tell her she has to start dating some other boys. This is ridiculous!"

"Give her time, Ned," her mother repeated. "She and Adam have been very close for a long time."

"I never really thought that was a good idea either," her father said. Then he allowed himself to be led into the kitchen to have a snack of turkey sandwich and left over pie.

Michelle pretended she'd just wakened when they returned to the living room. She sat up, rubbed her eyes, and asked what time it was. When she learned it was almost nine, she said she wanted to do some reading for school before she went to bed.

"Don't you want a snack?" her mother asked.

"I had too much turkey earlier," she said. That was not quite true, she hadn't eaten very much at all, but she wasn't hungry. Without Adam, the Christmas feast didn't taste right. Would he feel the same way about the fish he was probably eating right now?

Two days later, her mother spoke to her about dating other boys. Softly, she suggested, "You know, the time might pass more quickly for you if you were to go out with other boys."

"No one has asked me," Michelle said.

"Charlie Johnson asked you out New Year's Eve," her mother said.

"Mom, Charlie's the class clown."

"Susie says he's a nice boy," her mother persisted. "Isn't that so?"

"If Susie thinks he's so nice, let her go out with him," Michelle answered and got up to go to her room.

"Michelle!" Her mother's voice was stern. "Now we know that having Adam move away was difficult for you, but it's been a month and that's long enough for us to endure your moods."

"I'm sorry, Mother. May I go to my room now?"

Her mother sighed and nodded her head. Michelle went to her room and spent the rest of the afternoon reading a book and writing to Adam. In a way, she would be glad when school started again. At least it would get her out of the house for part of the day and away from her parents' worried eyes. And there would be schoolwork to do; that would take up some of the long, deadly hours.

When Susie came in later that day, Michelle accused her. "You've been talking about me behind my back," she said. "You told Mom about Charlie."

Instead of the response she expected from Susie, her sister nodded her head gravely. "I think you are taking this too hard, Michelle. I think you should start getting out more. Have some fun."

"I'm doing what I want to do," Michelle said.

"Is it because you promised Adam?" Susie asked. "I'll bet if you talk to him, you'll see that he's glad to let you off the promise. He probably wants to go out with other girls too, you know."

Michelle was ashamed to tell Susie that she'd never actually talked to Adam about dating other people. She knew they'd both carefully avoided the subject, but she wasn't sure why. She promised herself that she would talk to Adam about the pressure her folks were putting on her. Then she decided not to. As long as Adam didn't actually say he was dating other girls, she wouldn't bring the subject up. She'd already told him about Charlie's party and he obviously wasn't upset about that. She would just be more comfortable not talking about it at all.

"You could date a lot of guys, not just one," Susie suggested.

"Like you're doing?" Michelle teased. It was a good way to change the subject. For the last month, Susie had been besieged by phone calls from three different fellows. She was dating them all and obviously having a great time.

"And what about Derek?" Michelle asked. Susie had been out with the new boy who'd been at Charlie's Halloween party.

"I've only been out with him twice," Susie said. Then she frowned. "I may not go out with him much more. He's sort of . . . sort of aggressive."

"I know," Michelle said. "In fact, I almost warned you but I figured you could take care of yourself."

Then she added, "I wish you had the same confidence in me. Talking to Mom like that just made things worse for me, Susie. You should know that."

"I was just trying to do the right thing."

"That's what makes it so hard," Michelle sighed. "Everyone is so sure they are trying to do the right thing. Everyone is so sure they know what the right thing is. But it's my life and I've got a right to lead it my way."

On New Year's Eve, Susie went to Charlie's party alone because Michelle had a baby-sitting job. The ad she put in the paper brought an enthusiastic response and four people called her for New Year's Eve. The three she turned down said they would call her for other evenings.

Michelle spent New Year's Eve alone reading a romantic novel set in Elizabethan England. It was a good book and she didn't waste time feeling sorry for herself because she wasn't at the party. The money she earned that evening would go a long way toward paying off the money she owed for the telephone bill.

Susie reported the next day that Charlie seemed really downhearted because Michelle wasn't at his party. Susie didn't have a very good time at the party because she went with Derek, and they had a fight. She said, "My New Year's Resolution is never to go out with that creep again."

Michelle nodded her head. "Good thinking. Other than that, did you have a good time?"

Susie shook her head. "Not really. There was a lot of drinking and Charlie was pretty upset, I think. At least, he wasn't his usual cheerful self. It couldn't have been all because you weren't there."

"I don't think Charlie really cared that much," Michelle said. But it pleased her to think that there was someone who was interested enough in her to ask her to a party and then be sad when she wasn't there. But her thoughts were filled with Adam, not Charlie. She'd tried to call Adam several times the day before and the phone had been busy. Later, she'd tried from the house where she was baby-sitting and no one answered.

Now she was just waiting for noon so she could try Adam again. Noon in Wisconsin would make it ten in Santa Monica, a respectable hour for phone calls.

When Michelle called, Charlotte answered the telephone. When Michelle asked to speak to Adam, she said, "I hate to wake him; he was out late last night and he's still sleeping."

"Oh, did you go to a party?" Michelle asked. Though she couldn't honestly say she was crazy about Charlotte, she was anxious to keep their relationship smooth.

"I didn't go anywhere," Charlotte answered. "But Adam went with a girl from his school," she added pointedly. "It was nice of her to invite him and he wanted to go because he would meet people. I think he's really beginning to like San Diego High School. How are you doing?"

"Fine," Michelle said. "Tell Adam I called, will you? I'll call back in a few days. Goodbye."

When she hung up the telephone, she tried to tell herself it might mean nothing. Adam had a perfect right to go to a party, with or without a girl. He certainly would want to meet kids at school. She didn't want him to be lonely and miserable. But none of the things she told herself erased the dull ache in her heart. The idea of Adam at a party with another girl was really more than she could bear.

Michelle spent New Year's Day in her room writing letters to Adam. She tore them all up because, after all, there was nothing to say. They'd made no promises to each other about dating. They'd made no promises to each other at all. Finally, she wrote a newsy letter and made no mention of the fact that Charlotte had told her about his date. As she licked the envelope and put the stamp on it, she looked down at the pearl ring she was wearing on her finger. For the first time, she really questioned herself about Adam's love for her.

She was writing him almost daily but he seldom wrote. He said it was because he wasn't much of a writer but that he loved getting her letters. She was making all the phone calls but that was because he was supposed to be saving his money to come to Wisconsin this June. But would Adam really get to Wisconsin? There was always a doubt in his voice when she spoke of the future. Was the doubt about this summer or about *all* the plans they'd made?

When she called Adam three days later, he made no mention of the New Year's party and neither did she. They talked of his new job; he was working as a bus boy in the supermarket near their apartment. Michelle said, "That means you can really come to Wisconsin this summer. It will be so great to be together again."

"Michelle," Adam began slowly.

Michelle's breath caught; her stomach felt as though it was sinking down to her knees. She was afraid of what was coming.

"I'll try to make it, Mitchy. But you know, there's a good chance I won't be able to. Mom and I are going round and round about college. She says I can go to school here for free. I say I'm going back to Wisconsin. I don't know how it's going to work out."

"I see," Michelle said. She didn't see at all. Adam had never been able to stand up to his mother and now it sounded like he was giving in to her again.

"Just don't count on it, Mitchy. I'm just not sure I can swing it."

"Let's not talk about it now," Michelle said. She was fighting the feelings, battling the despair that wanted to drown her. "Let's just talk about happy things. I'll tell you about the A I got on my history test. Now, what happened to you that's happy?" There was a catch in her voice. For once, she was glad that Adam couldn't see her. She didn't want him to know how hurt and disappointed she was. If Adam knew that, he might feel sorry for her. If there was anything she didn't want, it was that.

In the evening, Michelle called Charlie Johnson on the telephone and asked him for the assignment in English class. She knew what the assignment was, but she just needed to hear a friendly voice. Charlie seemed pleased to hear from her and they chatted for awhile. Then he asked, "How's Adam?"

"Fine. He's got a job in a grocery store," Michelle replied.

"You two still going long-distance steady?"

Michelle held her breath for a moment before she replied, "Yes, we are."

"If you ever reconsider that decision," Charlie said in his most formal voice, "I do hope you'll alert me to the change in my prospects."

"I will," Michelle promised. "You'll be the first to know." When she hung up, she felt better, just to have talked to someone who liked her. Charlie could never replace Adam, but he was a nice boy.

Six

Susie got two boxes of candy and three valentines on Valentine's Day. Her father bought a five pound box of candy for his wife and large lollipops for each of his daughters.

"Lemon lollipops?" Michelle asked as she took a big lick off the giant sucker with the yellow ribbon. "I'd never pass this up."

Her father hugged her and kissed the top of her forehead, saying, "Enjoy yourself, kiddo." Then he went out to the office where he was busy preparing the materials for his income tax statement.

Michelle followed him into the office a few minutes later to ask, "Do you want me to help?"

"Not much you can do."

"Last year you asked me to look through the canceled checks," she reminded him.

He grinned and stretched, rubbing his eyes

and taking a sip of coffee all at the same time. "I forgot that. Sure, you can help if you want. Bored?"

"Sort of," Michelle admitted. She did not add that she was awfully disappointed that Adam hadn't even sent her a card.

Together, they looked through the stacks of canceled checks for those items that might be deductible. Her father, who was usually cheerful, seemed to be in an exceptionally good mood. He joked a lot as he worked and Michelle guessed that going through his books had told him he'd had a very good financial year. It was a nice, comfortable feeling to work beside her father.

Later, he said, "You're good at this. Ever think of studying accounting? You've got the head for it."

She didn't reply that she would study teaching to work with Adam. Those dreams didn't seem nearly as attainable as they once had. She just smiled and asked, "Think you'd like me to do your taxes?"

"Better yet, why not study creative writing?" he asked. "A little imagination never hurt a tax accountant."

"Oh, Dad," she repeated, laughing as she protested, "Stop the bad jokes."

Before he could think of a good retort, her mother called out, "Michelle, there's a flower here for you."

Michelle jumped up and dashed into the kitchen where her mother stood holding a single red rose. "Isn't it lovely?" she asked

67

as she held it out to Michelle. Then she warned, "I don't think it's from Adam. It was a local delivery."

Michelle hardly looked at the rose; she ripped open the envelope and read, "For the girl of my dreams. Love, Charlie."

"Charlie," she said as she put the rose down on the kitchen table.

"It's a pretty rose, isn't it?" her mother asked.

"Yes," was all that Michelle answered. Then she went back into the office to work with her father. No sense talking about the disappointment she felt. There was nothing to say.

Adam's valentine came a day late. It was a small card and the message was simply, "Love, Adam." Michelle was angry and disappointed and decided to call Adam and tell him how she felt. But when she called during the next three days, Adam was out or the phone was busy. She talked to Charlotte twice and on the third time, she said, "Look, tell Adam I'll call him Saturday night at ten."

Michelle chose Saturday night because she knew the grocery store where he worked would be closing early that night. In the back of her mind, she was also hoping to make sure that Adam would stay home on Saturday night, as she was doing.

But when she called on Saturday, it was Charlotte who answered the telephone. She said, "Adam said to tell you he'd be home tomorrow morning around ten or eleven. He's gone to a party tonight."

Michelle's face flushed and she felt a rush of body heat. Her stomach was in turmoil and her voice was choked as she said, "Tell Adam to call me." Then she hung up the telephone before Charlotte could say anything else.

Michelle sat on the edge of her bed, clenching and unclenching her fists. Then she turned to her pillow and began beating it. She didn't know who she was mad at, exactly. Charlotte or Adam? Or even herself? But the anger was real and it was strong. She shook as she beat the pillows.

So she didn't hear when Susie knocked on her door and then opened it. Her younger sister stood in the doorway looking at Michelle vent her anger. When Michelle saw her, she collapsed on the bed and wept. Susie came over and sat on the side of the bed. Taking her hand, Susie asked, "What happened?"

"Nothing."

"Did you talk to Adam?"

"No."

"Something must have happened to make you this upset."

"Nothing," Michelle sobbed.

Susie said, "Mitchy, you've got to do something about the way you feel. Adam's been gone for months and you're still not over it. That isn't like you."

"Go to bed," Michelle said dully. "I'll be all right in the morning."

"Do you want something? Some tea? Chocolate?" Susie offered. When her older sister didn't answer, Susie went to her own room without another word.

The next morning, Michelle stayed in her room as late as she could so no one would see her swollen eyes. When she went down to breakfast at ten, she looked fairly normal. However, she could tell by the look on her mother's face that Susie had already told her about the night before.

Her mother looked up from the Sunday newspaper and said, "We didn't call you because you needed the rest. There's still time to dress for church. Want to go with me?"

Michelle shook her head. She and Susie had never been forced to attend church with their mother. Since their father was not a church-goer, they'd always had the option of staying home with him and starting Sunday dinner. But now her mother urged, "It will make you feel better."

"I feel fine," Michelle answered, trying to make her voice match her words.

"We'll talk about that when I get home," her mother said. "I hope you're not planning anything for this afternoon?"

"No."

"Well, don't. Family conference time." Her mother kissed her and went out the door before Michelle could object.

Michelle started dinner that morning. She did it partly to try and convince her parents that she was all right, despite anything Susie might have said. She also did it because cooking was a simple activity, one she could do while she worried about other things. She tried to concentrate, but she knew she was waiting for the telephone to ring. When would Adam call? Surely, Charlotte would have told him she was upset. And Adam would care enough to call soon and try to talk to her. True, he was saving money, but her feelings would come first — wouldn't they?

Susie was obviously avoiding her. She stayed in her own room until their mother came home from church. Then, when her father called her to come down and help set the table for Sunday dinner, there was nothing she could do but come down the stairs and into the kitchen where Michelle was waiting for her.

"Thanks a lot," Michelle said sarcastically.

"I was only trying to help," Susie said.

"You make it worse, Susie. You make them worry more. Then they bug me."

"No," Susie said suddenly. "I'm not the one who's making it worse. You are."

Again, Michelle felt the anger boil through her body. She was amazed to experience it twice in less than twenty-four hours. Even while she raged inwardly, she was observing this new Michelle, learning about the depths of her emotions. She said, "Susie, if you want to be my friend, you'll have to learn to mind your own business."

But Susie, who had always been so eager to please her older sister, and who had always tried to imitate her as closely as she could, stood her ground. "I'm not your friend — I'm your sister. I did what I thought was best."

Suddenly, the anger toward Susie collapsed. Michelle felt like a very young girl again; she asked, "Do you know what the family conference is about?"

"You, I guess," Susie answered and turned to the cabinet to begin pulling out plates and glasses for Sunday dinner.

The meal was strained and there were long silences. Sometimes Michelle wished her family could yell and shout like other families did. She could barely remember a time when her parents had expressed anger toward her or Susie. They hadn't spanked her since she was three and that was to teach her not to run into the street. But in their own way, the Karlsens were very strict parents, with rules and expectations.

Family conferences were for serious matters. And this family conference was going to be about what was wrong with her.

Michelle sighed and stirred the apple pie around on her plate. Her mother asked gently, "Aren't you enjoying your own pie, Michelle?"

"I'm not hungry," Michelle said. She pushed back her chair and asked, "May I be excused?"

Her father nodded his head and Michelle rose from the table. As she left the room, she heard him say, "That's what gets me. She isn't eating anything."

Michelle went into the living room and waited, thumbing through a magazine. It was Susie's turn to do dishes and on some Sundays, she might have helped her sister, but not today. She didn't feel like doing anything at all. With one ear, she was straining to hear the telephone. The rest of her body was on alert, waiting for the family conference that was coming. What could they do? Demand that she be cheerful? Insist that she be happy?

In a way, that was what they did. Her mother, father, and Susie all followed each other into the living room and sat down. There was a long, dreadful silence and then her mother began, "We want you to be happy, Michelle. You've always been such a cheerful, sweet girl and we're worried about you."

She waited expectantly for Michelle to answer. When Michelle said nothing, she went on. "As you know, we're very concerned about your mood change since Adam left town. It's natural to be sad when someone you're dating . . ."

"I love him," Michelle interrupted angrily.

". . . when someone you love leaves town," her mother went on smoothly. "In a way, it's a kind of death, and grief is normal."

"He isn't dead," Michelle interrupted

again. Everything her mother said was making her angry.

Her mother went on. "We find your grief excessive, Michelle. And we're wondering if there is anything we can do to help you get over it." Again there was a silence, and her mother seemed to be waiting for her to say something. But Michelle couldn't think of anything she could say that would help matters at all. What could her folks do? Call Charlotte and demand she let Adam return to Wisconsin? They would never do that.

After a few minutes of silence, her mother said in a very sad voice, "We're worried about you, Michelle. You're not eating and you're losing weight. You're sad most of the time. You're just not yourself. Your father and I had no idea how dependent you were on Adam. Of course, we knew you were very close, but it never occurred to us that you *needed* him this way. We thought you might like to talk to Steve Murdock a few times. Just to clear up some of these feelings."

Michelle stared at her mother. They wanted to send her to a psychiatrist! They thought she was crazy! She could hardly believe her ears. "You mean Dee Ann's father? But he works with crazy people."

"That's nonsense. He works at the hospital, and he sees private patients after hours. Your father and I would feel better if you saw someone we knew and trusted."

Michelle looked at her father and mother in dismay. Whose idea had this been? She looked suspiciously at her younger sister. Susie wouldn't look at her at all, confirming Michelle's suspicions. She shook her head and said, "I don't need to see a psychiatrist, you know. There's nothing wrong with me except I miss Adam. If Susie has been scaring you into thinking I'm nuts, don't listen to her. She worries too much."

Susie's head jerked up. She said, "You sure act nuts, Michelle. You never smile, you never have any fun. Even the kids at school have been talking about how changed you are. And you're missing cheerleader practice. Sally Nelson told me so."

Michelle shook her head. "Do you really think missing cheerleader practice is a reason to send me to a shrink?"

Susie said nothing more and her father smiled. He said, "We want you to get moving, Mitchy. We want to do whatever we can to help you get over this."

"Are you sure you wouldn't like to see Steve, dear?" her mother asked anxiously. "We're not going to force you, but sometimes it helps to talk to an outsider."

Michelle shook her head. She was thinking about the telephone again. She'd asked Charlotte to have Adam call her. But could she be sure Charlotte was really delivering the messages? Could she trust Charlotte? Or was that a crazy thought? Maybe Susie was right. Maybe she did need to see a shrink. Or maybe she should just try to call Adam again. All she wanted was for the family conference to be over. Then she would try calling Adam one more time.

"Perhaps we can make a plan that will be movement in the direction that we would like to see you go," her mother said. "What can you suggest?"

Michelle didn't answer.

"We're waiting for you to tell us what you're willing to do to get yourself back on an even keel," her mother said. This time, there was a firmness in her voice that Michelle recognized as a signal that something would be done. She had hoped that rejecting the idea of talking to Steve Murdock would end the conference, but apparently not. They seemed to have an agenda planned. It made Michelle angry to think that they had all been talking about her behind her back. She bit her lips and shook her head in silence.

"Susie thinks you should start dating," her father said. "I agree."

"Susie seems to be the one making the major decisions around here," Michelle said. She looked bitterly at her sister.

"We are a family," her mother said in that no-nonsense voice. "We care for each other and try to help each other. Your sister is trying to help you, as we all are. Don't take your anger out on her. Do you understand me?"

Michelle nodded her head. Why didn't the telephone ring? Why didn't Adam rescue her? She felt as though she wanted to go to bed and stay there for a week. Had she ever felt this way before? It was true, she had changed. No, that wasn't true. Before, when she and Adam were happy, there wasn't any reason to feel like this. She hadn't changed. The world had changed.

"We think it would be a good idea if you started getting out more," her mother said gently. "We'd like you to agree to go out with other boys if they ask you."

"No one will ask me," Michelle said. "They know that Adam and I are going steady."

"That's another thing," her father said. "We want you to tell Adam that you're not going steady anymore. We want you to tell him that you're going out with other people and he should, too."

Michelle stared at her father. How dare he tell her how to handle things between her and Adam? She sputtered, "You have no right . . ."

"If you don't agree to these terms," her mother said, "we're going to insist that you talk to Steve Murdock or someone equally qualified. We *do* have the right, Michelle."

"It's blackmail," Michelle objected. She rose to leave the room.

"Sit down," her father said. Usually, her father was a quiet, jolly man who let her mother do all the talking, but now he sounded just as certain as she did. He went on, in a softer but just as determined voice, "We have to insist on these things, Shell. We're going nuts watching you destroy your life moping about that boy."

"We want you to learn to take charge of your own life, and not depend on others so much," her mother added.

"It's not fair," Michelle protested. "You can't make me go out with people I don't want to."

Her father's face looked confused for a moment and Michelle thought he might waver. But her mother broke in, saying, "We've talked about this. While it doesn't seem fair, it's the best idea we've had. Do you have any others? Aside from letting things go on as they are, of course."

Michelle couldn't think of any better ideas because she knew there really weren't any. Finally, she said, "Just give me some more time."

"No," her mother and father said in unison. They had obviously been prepared for this plea. Her mother explained, "Adam left almost three months ago and we don't see any signs of improvement. At first, we thought you'd cry yourself out and get on with your life, but after Susie found you last night, it became clear that you need help moving on to the next step. Please don't blame Susie. You're lucky to have a sister who worries about you. And I'm sure if you're honest, you'll admit that you would be just as concerned about her if she were in your condition."

Michelle didn't want to listen anymore. She had a headache. She sat silently, pulling at the ends of her cut-off jeans. Her legs were cold and it had been silly to wear these short pants, even with her wool knee stockings. She knew she'd selected them because she wanted to believe that summer was nearer. But summer was a long way off and her knees were cold.

"So will you agree to start going out? I don't mean only with other boys, I mean with your girlfriends, too. I want you being active again."

"What else can I do?" Michelle replied sullenly.

"And you'll tell Adam that you're not going steady anymore?" her father added.

Michelle nodded her head. There was no way she wanted to admit, even to herself, that Adam was already dating other people. Or if he wasn't exactly dating, he was sure going to a lot of parties. Michelle felt as though the whole world was conspiring against her. She had lost this battle, she knew. In her heart, she was afraid she had lost much more. Would Adam take this new turn of events as a reason to move even farther away from her?

Her father added, as if reading her thoughts, "In case you're worried about losing Adam permanently because of these changes, I can only remind you that if he's that easy to lose, it would never have worked out anyway."

Michelle didn't acknowledge his words. She asked, "Are we finished? May I go now?"

"Not until you tell us what you intend to do about getting out more. We want a definite plan from you."

"I'll call Charlie Johnson and ask him out," Michelle said. At least Charlie was available and a familiar friend, she thought.

Her mother nodded, obviously waiting.

"And I'll get back to cheerleader practice."

"And start eating better," her father prompted.

Michelle sighed and nodded her head.

"We could go ice skating this afternoon," Susie offered. The shy tone of her voice made Michelle feel guilty. Susie sounded really worried that Michelle might be angry with her.

Michelle shook her head, rejecting the offer. The truth was that she *was* angry at Susie and her parents, but she understood that they loved her. When she saw the deep disappointment on Susie's face, she softened the rejection by saying, "I have homework to do and I have to call Adam and Charlotte."

Susie nodded her head and went to the closet for her ice skates. As she went out the door, she turned to Michelle and said wistfully, "If you change your mind, I'll be at the pond with Dee Ann and some other kids. You can come anytime."

The telephone rang then and Michelle raced to answer it, leaving Susie in the door without an answer. But it was a call for her mother. Michelle went to her room to think about what she was going to say to Adam. She also had to plan the best way to approach Charlie about a date. She would have to make it clear that dating him didn't mean she'd given up Adam. But Charlie would understand that.

As it turned out, she didn't talk to either Charlie or Adam that afternoon. She called them both but neither one was at home. However, she stopped Charlie in the hall at school first thing Monday morning and asked him, "Would you like to go out with me?"

"Are you kidding?"

"No, I mean it. My folks say I have to start dating someone and you're my choice. I mean, as long as you understand that Adam and I . . ."

"As long as I understand that Adam's first choice," Charlie finished for her. Then he smiled and said, "Second choice is a winning position too, Mitchy. Pick you up at seven?"

"Not tonight!" Michelle said in alarm. Then seeing the hurt expression on Charlie's face, she explained, "I baby-sit a lot and I have a job tonight. I just meant someday."

Charlie nodded and said, "How about if I call you tonight and we pick a someday."

Michelle gave him the number of the house where she would be baby-sitting and they separated. She was a little surprised at how good she felt about asking Charlie out.

That evening, Michelle tried one more time to get through to Adam. Charlotte's voice sounded snappy as she said, "You know he works on Monday evenings."

The familiar tears rose to her eyes as she said, "I forgot. Have him call me, Charlotte. Tonight."

"He won't be in till ten-thirty. That job is ruining his health."

"Have him call me. I'll be up," Michelle insisted. She supposed that Charlotte blamed the job on her, and she guessed that Adam and his mother were not getting along very well these days. But no matter what their problems were, Michelle felt such a strong need to talk to Adam tonight that she had to insist. Closing off, she said, "Please, Charlotte, it's important."

"I always give him your messages," Charlotte said defensively.

As Michelle hung up, she stared thoughtfully at the telephone. *Did* Charlotte always give him her messages? She would probably never know.

Adam called at exactly ten-thirty. Michelle raced through her news, telling him quickly about the family conference and her decision to start going out with Charlie. She said, "And my father says we can't go steady anymore. Whatever that means."

"I guess it means we're free to date other people if we want to," Adam said. His voice sounded tired and discouraged.

"Or even if we don't want to," Michelle said, trying to get a laugh out of him. "Are you all right?"

"Sure," Adam said. "The hours are long and Mom and I are going round and round again. But everything is all right."

"Is there a good time to call you?" Michelle asked. "I mean, the last three or four times I've called, Charlotte's answered."

"Maybe you shouldn't call as much," Adam said. "I'm not home very often these days."

"Adam . . ."

"What, Mitchy?"

"Adam, I want to call you. When is a good time?"

"Let's make it Sunday mornings from now on, Mitchy. I'll be home then and you will be, too. Okay?"

They agreed on that and talked for a minute or two about school, then Adam said, "Mitchy, I've been on the telephone ten minutes. I have to go."

"Forever," Michelle said, but Adam had already pulled the receiver away from his ear and she heard only a click in response.

Seven

Her first date with Charlie was fun. They went to a horror movie and laughed all the way through it. After the movie, Charlie took her to a McDonald's where kids from school congregated. Michelle had a few bad moments when she walked in the door with Charlie; it seemed strange not to have Adam by her side. However, the people who greeted them didn't seem to find anything strange about seeing her with Charlie. When Sally and Betty Nelsen invited them to join their group, Michelle slid into the booth with no self-consciousness.

The twins were double-dating two boys from Readstown and they seemed to be having a good time.

Betty asked, "You going to make cheerleading practice Monday?" There was a slight note of reprimand in her voice.

Michelle blushed and answered, "I'll be there, I promise. I'm not going to miss any more practices."

"That's good," Sally said. "We've got a new cheer we're working on that's a real killer. Think you're ready to do a backbend?"

The three girls talked about cheerleading for a few minutes until one of the boys from Readstown turned the conversation to football. Both boys were on the Readstown football team and they claimed they had a chance to beat La Crosse next season, even though they represented a school of four hundred and La Crosse had almost a thousand students.

"You play football?" Betty's date challenged Charlie.

"No."

"Basketball?"

When Charlie shook his head negatively, the boy pursued, "What sport do you play?"

"None," Charlie admitted. "I don't like competitive sports."

Both boys looked amazed and Michelle felt a little protective towards Charlie. Though she knew that sports were only games, in high school all the really popular boys played football or baseball. She was sure the boys from Readstown were wondering why a cheerleader would go out with Charlie. But she told herself that what they thought didn't really matter. If they knew Adam they would be impressed, but they had no way of knowing about Adam.

To change the subject, she asked, "What do you think the chances are of an ice skating party next March 20th? Do you think the river will be breaking up by then?"

"Why March 20th?" Betty Nelsen asked. She was obviously as interested in switching the subject to safer ground as Michelle was.

"It's my birthday," Michelle answered. Until that moment, she hadn't thought of celebrating at all, but now she found herself saying, "I was thinking of having an outdoor barbecue. Ice skating. Hot chocolate, hot dogs. Why not? People who are born in July always get to have barbecues."

"The ice won't hold," the tall boy from Readstown said. "It's usually broken by the middle of March."

"But this is already the first week in March," Sally said, "and it's really solid. Betty and I went ice skating yesterday. There were hundreds of kids skating."

"If you really want an outdoor party," Charlie said, "We could have it on my farm. It's on the outskirts of town, towards Westby. There's a pond there and an old house."

"You mean your *folks* have a farm," the boy challenged Charlie. He seemed determined to put Charlie down and Michelle felt herself getting defensive for her date. She dropped her hand lightly into Charlie's and squeezed it as a silent signal that she was with him.

"It's my farm," Charlie said quietly. "I inherited it from my grandmother. Of course, I rent out the fields, but someday I'm going to live on it."

"In a deserted shack?" the curly-haired boy taunted.

Charlie said nothing more, merely biting into his hamburger. Following Charlie's lead, the other five applied themselves to the food in front of them.

Once or twice she glanced over at Charlie, wondering how he was feeling or what he was thinking. Though she couldn't actually say she was nervous about going out with him, there was something about dating a new person. Charlie could never compare with Adam, but she found herself wanting him to have a good time. Now, as she looked at him sitting beside her, she decided he was better-looking than she'd thought. Not that Charlie was handsome — he wasn't. Nevertheless, his high cheekbones, straight nose, and regular features were pleasant. His straight brownish-blond hair was cut too short, Michelle decided, but if he let it grow a little and if he would stand up straight instead of slumping, he would really be nice-looking.

Michelle realized that if she was thinking of suggesting that he let his hair grow longer, it meant she planned to see him again.

On the way home Charlie said, "It's a nice pond for ice skating and we could eat inside the house. I mean, if the weather is bad, it would be better than standing around with barbecue sauce freezing on your chin."

"Thanks for the offer," Michelle said. They

were drawing up to her house and she was feeling sad again. How very different a date was when it was with Charlie. The old longing for Adam returned. She felt like crying as they parked in front of her house. How many times had she and Adam parked in exactly this same spot. *If only Charlie doesn't try to kiss me,* Michelle thought, and she braced herself for the possibility.

But Charlie only took her hand in his and said, "I want to thank you for going out with me. I mean . . . I've always dreamed of taking you out but I never. . . ." Abruptly, he let go of her hand and said jokingly, "It was great. I wasn't even scared by the monster dragons with you beside me. You know, when I'm alone in those movies, I always hide my eyes."

"I had fun, too."

"Want to do it again?"

"Sure."

"Tomorrow?"

Charlie's eagerness both pleased and worried Michelle. She knew he had a crush on her and it made it easier somehow, to know that Charlie really liked her. But she didn't want to get too involved with him. Charlie was a nice guy and she didn't want to hurt him. Still, he knew about Adam and he seemed to accept the fact that she would always be Adam's girl. "I have to baby-sit tomorrow," Michelle said. "How about next weekend?"

Charlie nodded his head. "Want to double? We could drive to Madison."

"Three hours?"

"There's a good Mexican restaurant there."

"Oh," Michelle breathed in deeply, feeling the sharp pain of memory. She had gone to that Mexican restaurant on the day she'd said good-bye to Adam.

She shook her head. "Let's just go someplace around here. The Bodega, maybe."

"Want to double?" Charlie asked again. "Maybe see if Susie has a date?"

Michelle frowned into the darkness. She and Susie still weren't on very good terms. Though they were polite, the old closeness was gone. She felt everything she did or said around Susie had to be controlled for fear she would report to her parents. "No," she answered. "I'd just as soon go alone."

"Fine with me." Charlie's voice was enthusiastic.

Michelle opened the door quickly and slid out of the car. She said, "I had a nice time. See you in school."

Before he could get out of the car, she was on her front porch and opening the door with her key. Charlie watched from the car until she was inside the door and then he drove away.

The next morning at breakfast, her mother asked her if she'd had a good time. "Fine," Michelle replied.

Her mother nodded and suggested, "You might think of some other boys you'd like to date and invite them to your birthday party."

Michelle stared at her mother, then asked, "How many do I have to date?"

Her mother sighed and said in a quiet voice, "You don't have to date any number, Michelle. I just assumed you'd want to go out with more than just Charlie. You'll be doing the same thing all over again, depending on *one* person too much."

"I like Charlie."

"You said he was the class clown," her mother reminded her.

"That was a long time ago," Michelle said. "I mean, in the seventh grade, he played a lot of practical jokes. And then later, he made jokes. But he's a nice person. I like Charlie."

Her mother looked at her for a long time and Michelle expected that she would object, but she said nothing. Michelle began to get quite uncomfortable under her mother's gaze and dropped her own eyes to the breakfast table. If her mother didn't have any more to say, then neither did she. She asked, "Is there any more orange juice?"

"No, but there's grape in the freezer," her mother answered.

When Michelle came back from the kitchen with the grape juice, Susie was seated at the table. Michelle offered her some juice and said good morning very politely. Susie nodded and asked, "Where is the sports section?"

Breakfast was quiet. Susie read at the table and for once, her mother didn't reprimand her. Her father was still asleep or maybe he was in his bedroom, watching television. Finally, the silence got to be too much for

Michelle and she said, "Charlie asked me if I wanted to have my birthday party at his farm. We could use his ice skating pond and cook a barbecue in his farmhouse. He owns his own farm," she added lamely.

"That's nice," her mother answered. "Will it be a big party?"

"I don't know," Michelle said. She was already sorry she'd mentioned a party. She would be seventeen and that wasn't such an important year. Not like her sixteenth year, when they'd had a great big party.

"You make the list," her mother said. "Then we'll plan the refreshments. Susie will help, won't you?"

Susie didn't look up from the paper.

"Susie?" Her mother said in a louder voice.

"Sure," her sister said, still not looking away from the paper in front of her.

Michelle stood up to leave the breakfast table, but her mother reminded her, "Our agreement includes three meals a day."

"Mother, you talk like I'm anorexic or somthing. I've only lost five pounds."

"And when you put on that five pounds, we'll be happy," her mother replied, smiling.

Michelle sat back down and ate the scrambled eggs in front of her. Then she buttered a piece of toast and ate that. "May I be excused?" she asked. She looked at her watch. Ten o'clock here. That meant it was eight in California, late enough to call Adam.

Her mother nodded permission and Michelle left the dining room to go up to the telephone in the upstairs hall where she would have more privacy. As she climbed the stairs, she could hear her mother and Susie talking, whether about Susie's behavior or about Michelle's problems, she had no idea. *I don't really care either*, Michelle thought suddenly. *Whatever they have to say to each other is their business.*

Adam sounded happy and relaxed on the telephone, and for the first time in weeks, they had a decent conversation. She told him about school and about the horror movie she had seen the night before, leaving out the fact that she'd gone with Charlie. If Adam guessed, he didn't let on and Michelle thought that was just as well. If they were going to be dating other people, there was no reason to torture each other with the details.

"What are you so happy about?" she asked.

"Things are better here," Adam said. "Mom and I are getting along. She's happier at work and I guess I'm finally adjusting to the new school. It was hard, Mitchy. Everything was different and I missed you so much."

Michelle smiled; how like Adam not to say how much he missed her until the worst of the really tough times were over. She said, "I want you to keep on missing me, Adam."

"I will," he laughed. "I promise you that. But it's good to be comfortable again. I guess I've been as miserable as I've been since . . . since Dad died."

"I've never been this miserable before," Michelle admitted.

"But you're adjusting too, Mitchy?" His voice was anxious. "I hate to think of you being unhappy all the time."

"I'm doing better," Michelle admitted. Should she tell him she'd actually had fun with Charlie last night? Better not to. She did say, "I may have my birthday party at Charlie's farm this year. Ice skating."

"Ice skating," Adam said wistfully. "The weather here is weird. It's really too cold for swimming, but it isn't winter either. I wish you could see it. Fog all the time and it's damp, Mitchy . . ."

She waited with a lump in her throat. Whatever he said next would be important. At the same time, she rejoiced in her knowledge of Adam. How wonderful to know someone so well that you could tell by the very tone of his voice when the mood had changed to something serious.

"Mitchy, do you think you could come to California this summer?"

"I doubt it," she answered, tears welling in her eyes. He wasn't going to be able to manage to come to Wisconsin after all.

"Couldn't you at least ask them?"

"I'll ask, but I know the answer," she said. She didn't tell him that she now owed her folks close to two hundred dollars in telephone bills. It would only worry him and it wasn't just the money that would make them say no. They had their own ideas about what was and was not proper. Besides, she wasn't sure Charlotte would really welcome her visit.

"Ask them," Adam said quietly.

"You're not going to be able to come out, are you?"

"I'm going to try," he answered. "I'm working just as hard as I can to save money for school and for the trip but it isn't easy, Mitchy."

"It's only March," Michelle said. "June is a long way off. We'll think of something."

"Sure," he said, but some of the happiness was gone from his voice.

Michelle was sorry that their mood had changed back to sadness and she tried to lift their spirits by telling him about the weather in Wisconsin. "No fog here," she teased, "only snow. We've got about three feet on the ground and more coming. As for swimming weather, let me tell you, it hurts to walk more than a block. Last week, they closed school for two days. I feel so sorry for you out there in sunny California."

"I miss you, Mitchy. You'd better hang up now."

"I guess so. I'll talk to you next Sunday, Okay?"

"I'll be waiting," Adam said. Then he added softly, "Mitchy, hang in there. It won't be forever."

"Forever," Michelle said softly, and she hung up the phone.

E^{ight}

At cheerleading practice on Monday, Betty asked her, "You dating Charlie a lot?"

"That was my first date," Michelle answered.

"But you like him?" Betty pursued.

"He's nice." It occurred to Michelle to wonder why Betty was asking. Did she think Charlie was a funny person to be dating? Or did she want to talk about Adam's reaction? Whatever it was, Michelle decided to switch the subject.

"Will you show me the new routine before the others get here? I don't want them to be any madder than they already are about my missing practice."

"Don't miss any more," Betty warned. "Doreen's hoping they'll kick you off and Tracy Scott will get on." Then she made a mock shudder and said, "Ugh. I don't like Tracy at all."

"Me neither," Michelle admitted. "She always seems ready to make you look bad."

"Think of what she'd do for the squad."

"Not if I can help it," Michelle said smoothly and then said, "Come on, let's get to work."

The two of them worked for ten minutes before Doreen, Sally, and Beth arrived. By the time the other three girls were organized, Michelle had mastered the basic routine for the new cheer and was ready to go. Doreen had a new reggae record and she wanted to work out using that music. The other girls agreed, and soon they were bending, twisting, and jumping to the West Indian rhythm. After an hour, Sally called practice to a halt, saying, "Looks great. Michelle, it's good to have you back."

Michelle smiled and wiped her forehead with a towel. The exercise felt good and she realized that she really hadn't done much exercising this winter. Usually, winter was the time for ice skating and skiing. But she hadn't been ice skating once, and the cost of lift tickets made skiing out of the question. All her money was going for telephone calls these days.

Thinking of her tight budget, she turned down an invitation to go to Brewster's for a malt, saying, "I'd better study."

"Study later," Sally urged. "We can talk

about our new routine. It will be official business."

When Michelle changed her mind and accepted, the other girls, except Doreen, seemed pleased. Doreen said, "I promised to meet Tracy at four-thirty. So I guess I'll skip it." She seemed to be waiting for someone to suggest she invite Tracy to join them. When the silence persisted, Doreen said, "See you," and left the group.

At Brewster's, Sally said, "Doreen was really mad when you showed up today. She doesn't say much, but I think she's jealous of you."

"Why me?" asked Michelle. "I've never done anything to her."

"First she liked Adam, even though it was hopeless. Then she liked Charlie," Sally said. "And now Charlie has you."

"No he hasn't," Michelle said. "No one's got me. I'm myself."

"You can't say that a person's *got* another person," Betty corrected her twin. "But you can say that certain persons are *together*. Like Charlie and Michelle."

Why did the twins automatically assume that she and Charlie were a couple now? Didn't they know that she and Adam were in love? She wanted to interject a protest against their easy assumption but the conversation moved to another subject before she got a chance. Talking with the twins was like ice skating — you had to keep moving or you could lose your train of thought. The twins skimmed over subjects, jumping from one thing to another with the greatest ease. They covered schoolwork, the spring thaw, summer jobs, and the history term paper in three minutes.

It was after the term paper topic that Michelle learned Susie was dating Derek again. Sally said, "I guess your sister really likes him, doesn't she?"

"Why do you say that?"

"They were holding hands at lunch yesterday," Betty said, "and I heard they were going steady."

"He's too old for her," Michelle said. She didn't like the idea that Susie was going out with him. Hadn't Susie said that he was a creep? And why hadn't she said anything about Derek at home? Was she ashamed? Reluctantly, Michelle admitted that she and Susie weren't talking about much of anything anymore. But it wasn't like Susie to be silent about the boys she was dating. The small knot of worry lodged in Michelle's brain and she promised herself she would try to talk to Susie about Derek this evening.

That reminded Michelle that she should be heading home. She put her money on the table and told the girls good-bye.

It was a cold evening and Michelle shivered as she walked home, even though she was wearing wool pants and her down jacket. Wouldn't it ever be spring? It seemed as though the dreadful winter dragged on and

on. Tears were in her eyes as she tried to
figure out what had gone wrong this afternoon. They were nice girls; she liked Beth
and Betty and Sally a lot. Why hadn't she
been happier?

Michelle put her hands in her pockets and
hunched over as she walked into the wind.
She tucked her head down, hunching over
even more and hurrying home. She felt alone
and lonely and she supposed it was because
she still missed Adam so much. *If he had been
there this afternoon*, Michelle told herself,
I would have had a good time. If she hadn't
had any fun, she might have talked with him
about it. He would have helped her figure out
what was wrong. The truth was that if Adam
were here, she wouldn't care one way or the
other about a messed-up afternoon with the
girls.

Something inside her questioned this feeling, but she pushed it away.

When she got into the house, her mother
said, "Charlie called. He wants you to call
him back."

Michelle breathed the warm air of the
house and sniffed deeply, asking, "Cake?"

"Sweet rolls," her mother answered. "I
baked bread and some fancy pastries to
freeze."

"But we get some for dessert?"

Her mother laughed and hugged her as she
said, "It's good to hear you asking about
food. I guess your appetite is coming back."

For a moment, Michelle allowed herself to

lean her head against her mother's shoulder.
She breathed in the warm, homey smells and
felt, briefly, happiness. Then she said, "It's
cold outside," and walked toward the telephone in the hallway to call Charlie.

The telephone was ringing when she got to
it. It was Sally, who asked, "You and Charlie
want to come over tomorrow? We could
watch TV."

It wasn't until Michelle hung up the telephone and called Charlie that she realized
she'd answered yes for him the way she used
to answer for Adam. Even more disturbing
was the fact that she'd broken her promise
to herself and agreed to date Charlie more
than once a week. But when she heard the
eager acceptance in Charlie's voice, she
didn't worry any longer. It was nice to have
someone you could count on.

After Charlie agreed to the next evening,
he said, "I wanted to ask if you would go out
with me next Saturday night. It's kind of
important. My cousin is coming to town."

"Sure," Michelle answered. It seemed only
fair to say yes to Charlie. After all, he'd said
yes to her.

"This is a cousin who's about my age,"
Charlie said. "When we were kids, we spent
a lot of time together. He lives in California
now and I guess we've always tried to im-
press each other. But he was *always* a little
smarter, a little older than I was. I hope
we're past that. Anyway, I'd like you to
meet him."

She was really getting very fond of Charlie. Of course, he could never take Adam's place, but Adam wasn't here. As she hung up the telephone, she remembered the words to an old song she'd learned when she was a kid. "If you can't be with the one you love, love the one you're with." It was a silly song and Michelle was smiling as she hummed it to herself.

That evening, the dinnertime conversation was very lively. Her mother and father were discussing vacation plans for the next summer. Ever since Michelle could remember, her cousin Beatrice had spent two weeks at the Karlsen house in early July while Michelle's mother and father took a trip. Each year, the destination was carefully debated.

"I want to go to Amsterdam again," her mother said. "We didn't really get a chance to see the city when we were in Europe before. All those wonderful canals and I'd like to go to Venice this time."

"For the canals?" Michelle asked. "What's the big deal about canals?"

"Romantic," Susie answered. "She's a sucker for romance."

Her mother nodded happily and closed her eyes. "Venice and gondolas and then maybe up to Verona."

"Romeo and Juliet," Susie said to Michelle. "I think she really *is* feeling romantic."

"Why not?" her father asked. "We're only young once."

The idea of her parents as young made

Susie and Michelle smile at each other. "I'd go to London," Michelle said.

"I'd go to Rome," Susie said.

"I'm not going to Europe," her father complained. "Too crowded and too hot. I want to go someplace simple — maybe Alaska."

"Alaska's too big," her mother answered promptly. "Can't see Alaska in two weeks."

"Maybe year after this we'll all drive to Alaska," her father said. "Take a month or even six weeks."

Again, Michelle and Susie smiled at each other. Their father was always dreaming about a longer trip but it was difficult enough for him to get away for two weeks.

She felt very good to be sitting at the table with her family. She looked around the dining room at the soft gold wallpaper and the wide window with green plants hanging in front of it. Though it was still cold and snowy outside, it felt warm and summery in this room. Things really were all right.

After supper, she offered to help Susie with the dishes and her younger sister accepted with a surprised look. They'd been sort of avoiding each other for weeks. Once in the kitchen, Michelle said, "I heard you were dating Derek again."

"So what?" Susie's question seemed to break the lovely mood of the evening.

"So I thought you said you never wanted to go out with that creep again." Michelle didn't want to make things worse between herself and Susie, so she tried to keep her tone of voice as casual as possible.

Susie shrugged. "Derek's really a nice guy when you get to know him."

"Then why don't you bring him home so we can get to know him?"

Susie flushed and bit her lip for a moment. Michelle had the idea she was trying to decide how much to confide in her older sister. Finally, Susie said, "I guess it just hasn't been convenient."

"Susie, it's more than that," Michelle said. "You brought your other boyfriends home. How are you meeting him?"

For a moment, Michelle was afraid that Susie would tell her to mind her own business. *But this is my business*, Michelle thought. *She's my sister*. Then it was her turn to flush as she realized that Susie had felt the same way about her when she'd tattled about her hysterics that night. Michelle said, "I'm not going to tell on you, Susie. But I just want to help you if I can. Why don't you tell the folks you're dating Derek?"

"I made a big thing out of the pass he made that first night," Susie said. "Now I'm afraid if I tell them about Derek, they'll say I can't date him. You know how old-fashioned they are."

Michelle considered whether it was fair to call them old-fashioned. She supposed in some ways they were, but she was also sure that there was more to Susie's reluctance to tell them about Derek than that. "If you bring him around and they get to know him, they won't worry," Michelle said. "I think they'd worry more about you sneaking around with him."

The look on Susie's face closed as she said, "I'm not sneaking. Mostly, I see him at school. Besides, he's not anything like what you think. He's a very nice person."

"I'd like to get to know him better," Michelle said gently. She waited for Susie to respond.

But Susie folded the dish towel carefully and put away the last of the dishes. She said, "Thanks for helping."

"Maybe he'd like to double date with Charlie and me," Michelle offered.

"Derek hates double dates," Susie said quickly.

"Would you like to go out with Charlie's cousin next Saturday night?" Michelle offered. "I think that would be fun."

"I'm going to a rock concert with Derek," Susie said quickly.

"A rock concert?"

"In Madison," Susie answered. "It's all arranged."

Michelle could tell by the tone of Susie's voice that there wasn't anything else to say without making her mad again. She said, "If you change your mind, let me know."

"Michelle," Susie said later that evening as they were climbing the stairs to go to their rooms, "I have a favor to ask."

"Sure," Michelle asked. She expected Susie to ask if she could borrow something — a scarf or necklace since they were too different in size to actually exchange clothes.

"Don't tell the folks I'm going to the concert in Madison," Susie said. "I'm going to tell them I'm spending the night with Dee Ann. Actually, I am going to spend the night there. Dee Ann's folks don't care what time she comes in, so they'll let us go to the concert."

"But that's lying," Michelle said. She was surprised and a little shocked at Susie's deviousness. Was it Derek's influence?

"It isn't really lying," Susie said. "It's more like leaving part of it out not to worry the folks."

"Leaving out Derek and the concert is a pretty big part," Michelle said wryly.

"You won't tell, will you?"

Michelle wasn't sure what she could answer. On the one hand, she'd been furious with Susie for telling on her. She'd be a hypocrite if she turned around and did the same thing to Susie. On the other hand, she was really worried about what was happening with Susie. Sneaking around like that just wasn't right. She said, "I'll have to think about it. I'm not sure."

There was a plea in her sister's voice as

she said, "He's really a nice boy. I like him a lot." Then she added in a lower voice, "I think I'm in love with him."

"You're too young," Michelle said quickly. "You can't be in love at fourteen."

"You were," Susie reminded her.

"But that was different," Michelle said. "I've known Adam all my life. You don't know a thing about Derek except that he's the new boy in town. You have to be careful, Susie, you really do."

Susie shut the door to her room, leaving Michelle outside, looking at the brightly painted door with the KEEP OUT sign hanging on it. Should she break Susie's rule and force her way into her younger sister's bedroom to continue the conversation? Should she tell her parents how worried she was about Susie's behavior? Or should she do nothing and let things take their course? As always when she had a decision to make, Michelle missed Adam desperately. *Maybe I really was too dependent on him*, she thought. The idea bothered her more than she cared to admit and she went to her room determined not to worry about Susie's problems anymore. She would work on her homework and let Susie live her own life. After all, that was what she said she believed in, wasn't it?

N_ine

But Michelle changed her mind about not interfering the next morning. Susie was too important to neglect if she was sure she was headed for trouble. And Michelle was sure that keeping her dates with Derek a secret was trouble. So Michelle spoke to Derek at school the next day. "I hear you and Susie are going to a rock concert Saturday night. Why don't you change your minds and come to the movies with Charlie and me?"

Derek frowned and asked, "Who told you about the concert?"

"Susie did," Michelle answered. "Want to double date with us?"

"No," Derek said shortly and walked away from her. Michelle watched him disappear down the hall. Susie might say that Derek was a nice boy, but she didn't see any signs of it. As far as she was concerned, he was still a creep — a rude creep. *At least I tried,* Michelle told herself and went to English class.

That afternoon, Susie was home from school when Michelle got there. She was sitting in the living room, thumbing through a magazine. When Michelle entered the room, Susie looked up and said, "Well, I just wanted to thank you a lot. He broke the date."

"What?"

"He was so mad at me for telling you about the concert, that he broke the date. I guess you can tell yourself that you're even now." Susie's eyes looked red and swollen.

"Susie, I'm sorry," Michelle began. "But if he broke a date for that reason, then he really isn't right for you."

"You have no right to decide that!"

"Come with Charlie and me," Michelle urged. "His cousin might be nice. Forget Derek."

Susie shook her head stubbornly. She said, "I'm in love with him."

"If it really is love," Michelle said, "it takes two people. Does Derek love you?"

Susie began to cry again and she said, "I thought he did. I thought he was really interested in me. I mean, I liked being with him and all. I thought he felt the same way. But now I don't know."

Michelle slipped her arm around her sister's shoulder and said, "Forget him, Susie. Get out and have fun. Date some other fellows."

108

Susie managed a small smile and said, "Those are my lines."

"They're good lines," Michelle said. "They worked for me." As she said this, she wondered if that was really true. She wasn't really over Adam. She was in love with Adam. Susie's case was different. Her feelings for Derek were just infatuation. "Come on," she urged. "We'll have a great time Saturday night."

Susie nodded her head in agreement. "I guess so," she said. Then she turned to Michelle and asked, "If he dropped me for that, he really was a creep, wasn't he?"

Michelle nodded her head vigorously. She could see that Susie's good spirits were already returning. She hugged her sister again and then said, "What about tonight? Want to go to the movies or something?"

"I've got a date with Bailey," Susie said. Then she realized how silly that might sound after her dramatic scene and she laughed. "I guess I'll get over Derek, won't I?"

"Sure you will," Michelle promised, and she spent a few minutes congratulating herself on how easily the situation had been resolved. By direct action, she'd been able to avoid the conspiracy against her parents and she wasn't a tattletale. What was even better, she'd helped Susie see what Derek really was. She felt proud of herself.

The feeling was increased the next day when Susie told her that Derek had tried to make up and she'd given him the cold shoulder. "I just told him the truth, that I didn't want to go around with anyone who was so stubborn," Susie related. Then she added, "Besides, I'd already promised Bailey I'd go out with him on Saturday night."

"What about Charlie's cousin?"

"Oh, him," Susie said. "Well, Charlie can get someone else, can't he? I mean, he didn't ask for me in particular and Bailey did. Bailey is a very sweet person," Susie added.

"I know," Michelle teased, "and you're probably in love with him." She held her breath as she waited for Susie's reaction. It had been a long while since she'd been comfortable enough with her sister to tease her. Before Adam left, their relationship had been great, but that was a long time ago. Adam had been gone almost four months and things had been strained between Susie and her for all of that time. Suddenly, Michelle realized she missed Susie almost as much as she missed Adam. She drew in a sharp breath at the realization.

Instead of getting angry as Michelle feared, Susie grinned and said, "Probably I am in love with him, but I'll get over it."

Michelle was so happy to be back on good terms with Susie that she didn't even object when Charlie suggested he call Tracy Scott to see if she would double with his cousin. Later, he reported that she'd accepted, and Michelle voiced some of her doubts. She said, "I'm surprised she wanted to double with me."

"Why?"

"I don't think Tracy likes me very much," Michelle said.

"She said you were good friends." Charlie's voice was confused.

"Did she? I always thought . . . we've been in some classes together and we know each other, but I wouldn't call her a friend."

"How could anyone not like you?" Charlie asked indignantly.

Michelle laughed and said, "You're sweet, Charlie. You always say nice things to me."

"That's because I like you," Charlie said promptly. "Just like everybody else does — only better."

There was something about the way Charlie tilted his head as he waited for her response that reminded Michelle of an old floppy-eared stuffed dog that Susie had on her bed. Michelle laughed and when she saw Charlie's expression begin to change to disappointment, she stopped laughing quickly and said, "It will be fine. It will give me a chance to get to know Tracy better. And your cousin will probably like her."

"My cousin will like you," Charlie said. "But he won't get you."

"No one will *get* me," Michelle retorted. "If your trying to make him jealous, don't use *me*!" She smiled to soften the words.

But Charlie obviously didn't want to talk about it and he switched the subject to Michelle's birthday party that was coming up the next week. Michelle was a little worried about the way Charlie was going all out for the party. She hoped he wasn't doing too much for her and she didn't want to disappoint him in the long run. "You don't have to make the refreshments," she said. "Mom and Susie will do that."

"I want to," Charlie said, and the look on his face told her it was useless to argue.

Charlie's cousin, Pete, looked a lot like him only he was older, not as tall and thin, and quite handsome. While Charlie's eyes were round and blue, Pete's eyes were deep and darker blue and fringed with black lashes. Mostly, Michelle decided, it was the way they held their heads and bodies that made them seem so different. They both had good features and if Charlie ever put on a little weight, he would also be a very good-looking man. *Maybe he already is*, Michelle thought and took another look at her date. She was so used to the Charlie that she'd known as a kid that it occurred to her that she wasn't really seeing the man. If Pete was so very handsome and Charlie looked this much like him, then maybe Charlie was handsome, too. The idea amused Michelle and she was smiling as she got into the car beside Charlie and said hello.

"I'm not used to the idea of Charlie having a girlfriend," Pete said and smiled.

There was something in his voice that Michelle didn't like, a slight condescension, rather than a good-natured razzing. When he smiled, he had a way of holding his mouth too tightly, so that the smile looked forced. The only word she could think of was arrogant. No wonder he made poor Charlie nervous. Suddenly, Michelle leaned close to Charlie, kissed him on the cheek and said in a soft voice, "Hi, Charlie. I missed you." She let her voice soften into a caress and clearly signaled that she and Charlie were very close. Let Pete digest that, she thought, and leaned back to enjoy the evening.

Pete launched into a monologue about California living, comparing it to Wisconsin and wondering out loud why everyone didn't head west. He complained about the weather all the way to Tracy's house and as they pulled up to the curb in front of her house, he asked Michelle, "Have you ever been to California?"

"No." Michelle wished he would change the subject. Talking about California always made her unhappy.

"You'd love it," Pete assured her. "Sunshine all the time. Blue ocean. Blue skies. And beautiful girls. The whole state is full of beautiful girls." Then he added, "You'd feel right at home there."

"I have a friend who says there is a lot of smog and traffic," Michelle said. "He prefers Wisconsin." *At least I hope he does*, she added to herself.

Charlie seemed impatient with the conversation and said to Pete, "Aren't you going in for Tracy?"

113

"You go," Pete ordered. "You know her. I'll stay here and keep Michelle company."

Charlie obeyed without argument and the minute he left the car, Pete said, "So what's a beautiful girl like you doing in a place like this? How'd you and Charlie meet?"

Michelle decided she didn't much like Pete and his lines. She smiled in what she hoped was a polite manner and said, "Charlie and I are old friends."

"I knew it!" Pete said. His handsome brown eyes seemed to glint maliciously in the light of the street lamp. "You're just going out with poor old Charlie because you feel sorry for him. Maybe we should regroup." As he said this, he ran his hand along the back of Michelle's neck.

She pulled away. She wanted to answer in such a way as to put him in his place, but Tracy and Charlie were returning to the car. There were introductions and Tracy climbed into the back seat beside Pete. She said to Michelle, "This will be fun. We've never double-dated before."

Michelle was a little surprised that Tracy was so friendly. But if there was any ulterior motive, Michelle never discovered it. Finally, she decided that Tracy was just a different person outside of school hours. At school, Tracy often seemed preoccupied and withdrawn; Michelle had always thought of her as a snob. But tonight, Michelle saw her as a friendly and energetic person.

Michelle wasn't sure if Tracy liked Pete until much later in the evening. By then she knew that Tracy shared her opinion that Charlie's cousin was arrogant and self-centered. Pete had managed to let them know that he lived in a big house in Pacific Palisades, that his mother and father both had high-powered jobs and that he drove a Porsche. He also told them that his girl-friends were the prettiest girls at his school.

Tracy seemed to enjoy herself and not pay too much attention to Pete. She beat every-one very badly at bowling. Her scores were all over two hundred and no one else came close to her. Finally, Pete said, "That's enough of this, bowling is a silly game any-way. Anyone can develop skill."

"That's right," Tracy agreed mildly. "I learned to bowl in Sunday School. We have a league on Tuesday nights." She turned her back on Pete and asked Michelle, "Would you like to come with me sometime? It's fun."

"Sure," Michelle agreed. From that point on, the two girls talked to each other and Charlie a lot, and more or less ignored Pete. Later, Michelle invited Tracy to her birthday party and she accepted.

"I won't be here," Pete said, as though he had also been invited. "I'll be back in Cali-fornia, land of golden sunshine and golden girls." No one commented.

Later, when Charlie went to the men's room and Tracy was buying a Coke, Pete turned to Michelle and asked, "So are you going to tell me how you and Charlie got together?"

It was a repeat of the earlier conversation and Michelle decided that Pete was either forgetful or so self-centered he didn't listen.

"It was the other way around," Michelle assured him smoothly. "I was really lucky when Charlie asked me out."

Pete laughed in disbelief.

"You have no idea how popular Charlie is with the girls," Michelle went on. "They're all after him. Always have been. In seventh grade, we called him Adorable Charlie. I'm not the only one who's crazy about him."

Clearly, Pete didn't know whether or not to believe Michelle. During the rest of the evening, she caught him taking sideways glances at his cousin. Once, she saw him shaking his head as though arguing with himself about Charlie's attractions. However, she noticed that some of Pete's arrogance toward Charlie disappeared.

Charlie seemed to relax as the evening went on and by the time they left the bowling alley and went into the pizza parlor next door, he was his usual self, making jokes and laughing at life. Michelle was careful to keep her arm through his and lean her head on his shoulder from time to time to convince Pete that she'd been serious about what she'd said.

The obvious affection between Michelle and Charlie, plus Tracy's indifference to his

116

charms calmed Pete down a lot. As the pizza arrived at the table, he was acting more like an equal and less like he was slumming. The two cousins started talking about old times, when they had both been kids in Wisconsin.

"He was a cry-baby," Pete said of Charlie.

"That's because you were always beating up on me."

"He deserved it," Pete assured them. "One time he put a snake in my bed."

"You put a worm in my shoe," Charlie answered.

"You put a frog in my soup," Pete accused.

The outrageous accusations flew back and forth as Tracy laughed. Finally, Pete said, "Seriously, Charlie was a scaredy-cat. He cried every time he saw me."

"That's because you were always beating up on me," Charlie defended himself.

Michelle thought she detected a note of *real* defensiveness in Charlie's voice. Breaking into the conversation, she said, "They tell me I cried all the time until I was three years old. Funny thing is, I never cry now." As she said that, she remembered the last few months, when all she seemed to have been doing was crying. She grinned, "That is, I don't cry very much anymore. Not until I'm hurt."

"Pretty girl like you should never hurt," Pete said.

Charlie dropped his arm around Michelle's shoulder and said, "Hey, she's my girl." But underneath the protest, Michelle could see that Charlie was delighted that his older cousin found her attractive.

Tracy didn't seem to mind Pete's compliments to Michelle. It was pretty clear that Tracy didn't care enough about Pete to worry about anything he said. But she seemed to be having a good enough time and when they dropped her off at her door, she said, "It was great fun. I'll see you two at school on Monday." Then she took Pete's hand and said, "Don't bother coming to the door with me." Her last words were to Michelle. "Thanks for the invitation to your party."

But Pete was not so easily dissuaded. He jumped out of the car and put his arm around Tracy as he walked her to her door. Michelle and Charlie watched as Pete grabbed Tracy around the waist and bent her backwards for a good-night kiss. Then they saw the door open and Tracy slip inside. Michelle laughed softly and said, "Blind dates are often blind."

Charlie said, "Thanks for tonight, Mitchy. He was my idol when I was a kid. I guess he was just enough older to make it seem like I'd never catch up."

"You've caught up," Michelle assured him. "In fact, I'd say you were way ahead of the game."

Charlie dropped his arm around her shoulder and squeezed her to him. Michelle relaxed and let herself enjoy the warmth and comfort of leaning against Charlie's shoulder. It felt good to be sitting beside him, felt good to be next to someone as nice as Charlie.

When it was her turn to be dropped off at the house, Michelle said good-bye to Pete and then asked Charlie if he would call her tomorrow. In a soft voice, she said, "I want to talk about the party plans."

Charlie walked her to the door and Michelle held his hand, staying close to him so that Pete could see that they were touching. When they got to the door, she put on the porch light, as though she were looking for her key, then she raised up on tip-toes, put her arms around Charlie's neck and pulled him closer to her. "This is for your cousin," she whispered and lifted her head to meet his. The kiss was long and warm and though it wasn't the same as kissing Adam, Michelle enjoyed it. Standing in the circle of light, with Charlie's arms around her, she felt peaceful and friendly, as though she would never have to worry again.

Finally, they pulled apart and looked at each other. Charlie said, "This is for me," and pulled her close to him for a second kiss. This time, Michelle returned some of his intensity. When she pulled away from him, she was startled at how much she had enjoyed the kiss. She said, "'Night, Charlie."

"Mitchy . . ." he began.

But Michelle didn't want to hear what he had to say. She opened the door and said, "Talk to you tomorrow," then she ducked inside before Charlie could say another word.

On the inside of her house, she leaned against the door panel and stared at the empty house in front of her. The light at the foot of the stairs was on and the rest of the house was dark and silent. Everything seemed different in the dim light; there were shadows everywhere. What was she doing with Charlie? Why had she responded to his kiss like that? It frightened her to think about what a good time she'd had tonight. She'd been happy, really happy.

But, if she'd been happy, what was wrong with that? No one could blame her for enjoying herself, could they? "Adam," she whispered into the silent night, "Adam, I need you to come home."

Ten

Michelle woke feeling wonderful. She rose on one elbow and looked at the photographs of her and Adam all around her bedroom. There were dozens of them; the biggest was the formal portrait they'd had taken at her sixteenth birthday party last year. She smiled at the photo. Adam and she looked so happy together. She was wearing a pale blue dress and Adam had on his dark blue jacket. He was smiling that special smile that was halfway between his sweet smile and his joking smile. That had been last year, when she was sixteen.

She hopped out of bed, pulling on her yellow robe and running a comb through her hair. Then she quickly bent down and kissed Adam's image in the large photograph and whispered, "I wish you were going to be here, Adam. I really do."

But she did not linger over the photographs. There was too much to do. She was helping Charlie with the refreshments and, he would be here soon to take her to the grocery store. She showered, brushed her teeth and dressed in her Levis and pink sweater in a record five minutes. By eight-thirty, she was outside Susie's door, knocking and calling, "Wake up, sleepy-head."

"Happy birthday," Susie mumbled, and then there was silence. Michelle smiled at the closed door. She would let Susie sleep for a while and she and Charlie would come back for her after the trip to the grocery store.

Charlie was at the door before she finished her breakfast and Michelle greeted him happily, saying, "It's going to be a great day for a barbecue."

"Sure," Charlie agreed and then shivered. "It's already up to twenty degrees and the wind's only blowing at ten miles an hour."

Michelle laughed and poured Charlie some coffee. "You can't kid me," she said. "The weather forecast is for sunny skies and mild weather."

"In March in Wisconsin," Charlie reminded her, "mild means thirty or forty degrees."

"As long as it doesn't get too warm to melt the pond," Michelle worried.

"Don't worry about that," Charlie assured her. "I had Bert check it out yesterday and he says it's hard as nails. Pond's in the shadow of the hill, remember. And it stays cold."

"I've decided to let Susie sleep," Michelle said. "We can pick her up later. Okay?"

"Sure," Charlie agreed. "Gives me time with you alone. Nothing as romantic as the supermarket at nine o'clock on Saturday morning."

"No time for romance," Michelle teased. "We've got work to do."

"I still think you should have let me do it all alone," Charlie grumbled. "It's not fair for you to have to work on your own birthday."

Michelle's mother and father came into the kitchen then, and greeted Charlie, asking, "You're sure you kids don't want help with this party?"

"No thanks, Mrs. Karlsen," Charlie answered. "Everything's under control."

"Why don't you call me Christine?" Michelle's mother asked. "Looks like we know each other well enough by now for first names."

Charlie's face brightened and he nodded his head happily. Then he said, "You always seemed too young to be Mrs. Karlsen anyway."

Her mother laughed and said, "Flattery will get you a long way, Charlie."

Something about the warmth of her mother's tone made Michelle a little uneasy. She seemed so friendly toward Charlie, it was almost as if her mother had forgotten

Adam. Michelle stood up and said, "We'd better go to the market now."

Charlie seemed surprised but dutifully rose and said, "See you later, Christine."

As they were going out the door, her mother asked, "If you get any phone calls, when shall I say you'll be home?"

"I won't get any," Michelle answered quickly. She hated to have Charlie listening as she talked about Adam, so she didn't tell her mother that Adam had called last night to wish her a happy birthday. She was wearing his gift, a small silver bracelet that he'd bought in Ensenada, Mexico.

As they drove to the supermarket, Michelle chatted about Susie's newest love, Sammy Weiner. "She's known Sammy since second grade, but all of a sudden, she's discovered him. He's the best-looking, smartest, most wonderful boy in the world. I never knew anyone who could change as fast as Susie when it comes to boys. Last week, she was still after Tim Hardin, but this week, she only has eyes for Sammy."

"Your sister's young," Charlie said.

"It's more than that," Michelle said. "I honestly think she likes the excitement of having a million different boyfriends. I suppose it makes her feel popular or something."

"Maybe she likes variety," Charlie suggested.

"I guess so," Michelle said doubtfully. She couldn't understand the attraction of switching boyfriends every week. It had been difficult enough for her to get used to Charlie. The idea of dating a whole lot of different boys was too much to imagine. She said, "I just think it's a lot of trouble for nothing."

Charlie took her hand and squeezed it. "I'm lucky you're the faithful type."

The words bit into Michelle's heart. The faithful type? She was hardly that. Adam had been her boyfriend a month ago, but she was too honest with herself to believe that was still true. She was enjoying Charlie's company too much, and to be truthful, he was easier to be around than Adam was in some ways. Charlie was always cheerful and Adam had often been moody. Especially when he was fighting with Charlotte, Adam had been inclined to long, painful silences. With Charlie, Michelle never felt that sharp, anxious need to make things all right. Charlie was trying to please *her* and she had to admit, she liked that. *Why not?*, she asked herself. *I have a right to enjoy my life.* Behind the defensive thought was a deeper, more painful one. Adam had left her and though she knew he'd had no choice, she also knew she felt abandoned and a little betrayed by the loss.

She let her hand stay in Charlie's until they pulled into the parking lot of the supermarket. When they walked down the aisles of the supermarket, they held hands and pushed the cart together. They chose the cheese and lunch meats that would make up the sand-

125

wich plate together, but Michelle suggested they split up for the rest of the groceries. She could select the vegetables for the salad while he picked out the breads, but Charlie shook his head and said, "It's more fun this way."

"It's faster the other way," Michelle said.

"Yeah," Charlie agreed. "But this way, I can pretend we're an old married couple walking down the aisle."

Michelle drew in a sharp breath. Was Charlie serious? He must know that she wasn't thinking in those terms about him. She looked anxiously at him and tried to think of the right thing to say.

He looked down at her sadly and smiled, "Don't worry. I'm only dreaming. I know you wouldn't be interested in me for life."

"Charlie, don't say things like that," Michelle said.

"If only I were a frog," Charlie said in a hoarse voice as he bent his knees and rolled his eyes upward. "If only I were green and scaly instead of purple and slick. If I were a frog, I could get the beautiful princess to kiss me and everything would be all right. But, being a dragon, and breathing fire, I could not hope . . ."

"Charlie, don't be silly. People are looking."

"Naturally," Charlie said, as he straightened up and began pushing the shopping cart quickly down the aisle. "A princess like you must be accustomed to being stared at, especially if you insist on keeping company with purple dragons who breath fire. See that sign over there? Want to bet I can knock it over with one whiff of my ferocious breath?"

He moved up to a cardboard sign advertising mint cookies and huffed and puffed furiously. Michelle laughed and pulled on his arm, saying, "Be serious, Charlie. We've got a lot to do."

"I am serious," Charlie protested.

They finished the shopping quickly and were back at Michelle's house by eleven o'clock to pick up Susie. When they went in the door, Susie said, "You two look happy."

"It's my birthday," Michelle said. "Come on. We'd better get to the farm and get to work. They'll be there in a couple of hours."

"Sammy's coming with us," Susie announced. "We already put stuff in his car."

"But I thought you invited Tim to the party," Michelle said.

"I did," Susie admitted. "I also invited Bailey and Johnny." Then she added doubtfully, "I guess I'll have to circulate."

In some ways, the party was as much Susie's as it was Michelle's. She looked beautiful in her plaid wool slacks and her purple turtleneck sweater. Her long blonde hair was piled into a topknot on top of her head and when she skated, she wore a pink stocking cap with a purple tassle. The boys who surrounded her didn't seem to mind sharing her; apparently they were happy to be close to her at all. For a while, it looked as though Sammy was the real favorite of the afternoon, but later, Tracy brought her brother who was a freshman in college to the party.

"I hope you don't mind," Tracy asked anxiously. "He sort of invited himself and I needed a ride out here."

Michelle assured her that her brother was welcome and steered Tracy toward the refreshments. She noticed with an amused smile that Susie was doing her best to make the older boy welcome. Within ten minutes, she had him eating marshmallows out of her hand and then the two of them were skating arm in arm while poor Sammy looked on in dismay.

"Your party is a success," Tracy said.

"Yes," Michelle agreed. She looked at the outdoor barbecue where a group of kids were clustered as they roasted hot dogs. Then she looked down at the pond where others were skating. Their bright costumes seemed like flashes of summertime against the bare white winter landscape. Other kids sat inside the farmhouse, toasting themselves and marshmallows on the fireplace hearth. Michelle said, "Everyone seems to be having a good time."

Tracy ran to her brother's car. When she came back with a square package, she said, "Happy birthday."

Michelle undid the pretty pink flowered paper and was surprised to find a small book inside. Opening it, she turned to the first page and saw that Tracy had written, "This is your special book. For your own special hopes and dreams. Best wishes, Tracy." The rest of the pages were blank.

"I thought you might like to write something in it," Tracy said. "Poetry, maybe. Or just whatever you want."

Michelle was pleased by the gift and told Tracy that she would use it. "I'll try to think of something wonderful to put in it. Maybe I'll collect poems I like and copy them into the book."

"Why not write your own?" Tracy suggested.

But Michelle knew she would never be a poet. She would use the book for many things though. When she got home, she'd paste in the letters and cards that Adam had sent her from California. Should she make it just for the things Adam sent? No. She would also paste the Valentine card and notes that Charlie sent her. She was no longer *just* Adam's girl. She was an independent person with many friends of her own. It surprised her to realize that since Adam had left town, she'd made several new friends.

Following up this thought, she asked Tracy if she could go bowling with her next Sunday evening and Tracy readily agreed. Then Tracy picked up her skates and said, "I want to skate before dark. Besides, I'd better see what's going on between my brother and your sister."

Michelle made it a point to talk to all of her guests that afternoon. She went from group to group, sampling their conversations and staying long enough to let them know she was glad they were there. In a way, she enjoyed this party more than any party she'd ever had. In the old days, she and Adam would have held hands in the corner and watched people. Now, she was a part of the activities in a new and special way. As she laughed and talked with everyone, she realized she was really having a very good time.

Susie broke away from her admirers on the skating pond at about six o'clock and came back to the farmhouse to clean up.

Even as she offered, Tracy's brother came up behind Susie and asked, "Want some help?"

Michelle smiled and left them in the kitchen collecting dirty plates. It was nice of Susie to offer to help but she really didn't need to circulate among the guests anymore. She'd done her duty to everyone but her host. She hadn't seen Charlie for more than an hour. She decided he was down by the pond and pulled on her heaviest sweater so she could walk down that way.

As she walked, she thought about Susie. *Things are really O.K. between us again.* The knowledge made her happier than any gift she could have received.

Only a few people remained on the pond. By now, the air was so cold that they looked pretty uncomfortable. Michelle laughed and said, "Go inside where it's warm, dummies.

No one has to stay in this cold just because it's a barbecue."

The three remaining guests took her words as the impetus for moving toward the house. As they walked back, Michelle asked, "Anyone see Charlie?"

"He said he wanted to look for ice skates in the attic," Ted answered. "But that was an hour ago."

When they entered the house, Michelle asked the others, "Anyone know where Charlie is?"

"He's in the attic," Tracy answered.

"The attic?" Michelle repeated. She couldn't imagine why Charlie would disappear into the attic during his own party, unless he was angry or something. But that was so out of character that Michelle didn't really believe that could be the reason. "What's he doing in the attic?"

"Said he was looking for something," Susie said. "He came down a minute ago for a flashlight. Said to tell you where he was."

Obviously, Charlie wanted her to join him in the attic, Michelle decided. She wasn't too happy about climbing all that way to see someone who should be downstairs entertaining his guests, but she started up the stairs. Where was Charlie's famous party-giving talent? He was supposed to be the perfect host and now he was wandering around his attic, all alone.

The stairs were steep between the first and second floor and even steeper up to the attic.

They creaked, announcing her arrival before she called out, "Charlie?"

Charlie was sitting on a wooden box, digging through a pile of old clothes.

"I hoped you'd come up. I'm going through some old stuff that came with the farm," Charlie said.

"This farm belonged to my mother's grandfather," he went on. "When I inherited it, I was only three years old. They sold off all the furniture and paintings and stuff, and I've always been sorry about that. I guess I've always dreamed of living here sometime. Or at least having it for a weekend place."

"It's a pretty place," Michelle said. Then, because the house was small and not very special, she added, "I mean, the grounds are really nice. The pond and all."

"The house could be changed," Charlie said eagerly. "I think I'll knock out the walls between the bedrooms and make two big rooms. Then we could add a wing on the back." He stopped abruptly and smiled. "I guess you don't want to hear any more of those kinds of plans today, do you?"

"Charlie, I'm too young to be making plans like that," she said gently. "I want to go to college. And you want to, too."

"I'm not going to college," Charlie said. "I've decided to farm instead."

"But you told me yourself this farm isn't good enough to support a family," Michelle said in surprise. The idea of Charlie as a farmer struck her as funny. Charlie was tall, but he wasn't very athletic. And he didn't seem very practical either. She saw Charlie as too much of a dreamer to be very good as a farmer. Gently, she said, "I think you'll end up using this as a weekend farm. Maybe you could keep a few animals and live here. Your Dad will expect you to go into business with him."

"No," Charlie said. "I won't go into the sales business. Flying around selling machinery is no way to live. I wouldn't leave my family that way. My Dad isn't home half the time."

Michelle reached over and took Charlie's hand. She said, "Let's go down to the party. I'll come back with you tomorrow and we can sort this stuff out. If you really want to sell it, I mean."

"I might as well sell it," Charlie said. "The money in the bank would help me start my farm."

There was something sweet about Charlie this afternoon. She felt very tender toward him. Michelle had always known that beneath Charlie's cheerful exterior he was very lonely, but today he was really showing her that side of himself.

Taking his hand, she rose to her feet and pulled him up, saying, "We can come back tomorrow and look around. Remember there's a party going on."

"I know," Charlie said. "But I wanted to trick you into coming up here. I figured you'd miss me eventually and follow me. I've got a surprise for you."

He handed her a tiny package and smiled. "The attic seemed like the best place to give it to you. It's old and sort of a family treasure."

She laughed as she protested, "Charlie! You already gave me this party as a present."

"This is special."

She opened the small, tissue paper-wrapped package. Inside lay a small gold chain and an old-fashioned heart-shaped locket. It was tiny and adorable and she was sure it was very old. "It's beautiful," she said in awe.

"Open it," Charlie demanded.

Michelle found the little clasp on the heart-shaped locket and pushed on it. Immediately, the locket sprang open and she was staring at two side-by-side photographs. One was of Charlie and the other was of herself. Michelle didn't know what to say. The photographs staring up at her as a couple frightened her. She knew the locket was probably very valuable and she didn't know how to tell Charlie she couldn't accept his gift. Yet, she felt she shouldn't accept such a gift because it implied a feeling between them that wasn't there for her. She gulped and repeated, "It's very beautiful."

"It was my mother's," Charlie said. "And before that, it was my grandmother's."

Michelle's heart sank. To take the locket was unfair to Charlie. To return it would break his heart. Unconsciously, she twisted Adam's ring on her finger. Could she wear Adam's ring and Charlie's locket at the same time? But how could she give the locket back to Charlie without hurting him terribly?

Dazed by the complexity of the situation, Michelle said, "Thank you."

"Don't I get a birthday kiss?" Charlie asked.

Michelle turned toward him, raised up on her tiptoes and smiled at Charlie as she put her arms around his neck. "Of course," she said. But as she kissed Charlie, she felt only guilt. Was she being unfair to him? Or was it Adam she was being unfair to? Or was it to both of them?

E_leven_

From the night of her birthday on, Michelle
wore Charlie's locket around her neck and
Adam's ring on her finger. Whenever she
tried to think about the two men in her life,
she only felt confused and troubled, so she
learned not to think about it very much.
Charlie was always available, always at her
side. She liked Charlie a lot and there were
times when her feelings for him seemed
almost like love.

Adam seemed farther and farther away as
the weeks went by. She still called him once
a week and their talks were full of nice
words, but they seemed to have less and less
to share about their daily lives. Adam said
he was too busy working to have much to
report. Michelle said her life was dull, but
the truth was that too much of her life re-

volved around Charlie. She didn't mention Charlie to Adam and he never talked about any of the girls he might or might not be dating. They still talked of the future, but that future seemed very far away. Michelle realized that she had begun to believe it would never come.

Often, Michelle would look in the mirror and wonder exactly who she was and what she wanted. Her clear blue-eyed gaze never gave any clues. When she was with Charlie, she was happy enough. When she talked with Adam on the telephone or wrote him a letter, the deep yearning for his company surfaced and frightened her. She tried not to think too much about Adam these days because it only made her feel terrible. It was much easier to laugh and be happy with Charlie.

There were times when all she felt for Adam was anger at his desertion. The raw anger frightened her almost as much as the pain of loneliness. Sometimes, the anger bubbled up, causing trouble between her and Adam.

About two weeks after the birthday party, Michelle was talking to Adam on the telephone and he said something about a possible summer job. "But you're coming here this summer," she protested.

"Mitchy," Adam said in an exasperated voice, "I told you I may not be able to make it. Or, I may work most of the summer and come out the last part of August."

Because she was normally such a calm

person, her anger always surprised her. It seemed to erupt from such depths and seemed so out of control. When the anger was in charge, Michelle felt as though she was absolutely at its mercy. The energy behind her anger always seemed so much stronger than she was herself. Now, she said, "If you can't get here this summer, it's all off between us."

"Mitchy, you don't mean that."

"I mean it," Michelle said fiercely. "If you loved me, the most important thing in the world would be to be with me. I mean that, Adam."

Adam's temper had always been quicker to surface and he said, "You're being unreasonable."

"What's unreasonable about being with the person you love?"

"Don't act like a child, Mitchy. I'm doing the best I can."

"Are you?" Michelle asked. "Well, it's not good enough." She hung up the telephone and ran out of the house before he could call back. Michelle spent most of that Sunday morning walking through the park and feeling sorry for herself. She was also a little ashamed at her outburst when she returned home and learned that Adam had called twice. The phone calls were whittling away his precious money. And he needed that money for the trip east. But he wasn't coming east, Michelle reminded herself. So she decided to let him call her again if he wanted to make up.

Adam did call at two o'clock, when he knew the whole family would be sitting down to Sunday lunch. His first words were, "I don't want to lose you, Mitchy."

"You haven't lost me," Michelle said, but she felt very distant from him. The anger, now cooled, seemed to have moved her even farther away from her love for Adam. Did she really love him? Would she really ever feel the same way about him again?

"I just want you to understand that I'm doing the best I can," Adam said. "I don't want to lie to you. I don't want to make promises I can't keep, but I am trying, Mitchy."

"I know you are," Michelle said. But she wondered if she really did believe that. Was Adam doing the best he could? Or was he enjoying California too much to worry about getting back to Wisconsin? And how much influence was Charlotte really having on him, now that she had him out there alone with her? "I miss you," Michelle said. That much was certainly true.

They talked only a few seconds more and Michelle promised to call him again next Sunday. Once she hung the telephone up, she sat and stared at it a long time. She felt drained, worn-out, as though talking to Adam was very, very tiring. Once, her love for Adam had seemed a life-giving emotion. She had gained joy and energy from that love. Now, it seemed that all Adam had to

give her was pain. Slowly, she dialed
Charlie's number. Talking to Charlie would
make her feel better. Maybe she would even
invite him to come over later. They could
take a walk or watch television or something.

By the end of April, she was spending as
much time with Charlie as she used to spend
with Adam. They saw each other at school
and every afternoon he walked her home.
Most nights, he came over to her house to
visit or they went somewhere together. She
began to turn down baby-sitting jobs to do
things with Charlie. The phone bill was
almost paid off now and there wasn't really
any reason to hunt for more baby-sitting
work.

Charlie seemed very happy to be at her
side and seldom pushed her to demonstrate
more love for him than she felt. He obviously
adored her, but usually managed to joke
about it, rather than come on seriously.

No one talked much about Adam anymore
and most of the kids at school assumed that
Charlie was her boyfriend now. The invita-
tions came for Charlie and her both. The
assumptions about the future included
Charlie, not Adam. Michelle felt herself
slipping into a comfortable rut with Charlie.
He didn't make her feel as deliriously happy
as Adam had, but he never gave her pain.
Anything that she wanted to do, Charlie was
willing to go along with.

Sometimes, alone in her room, she questioned what she was doing. Was she just

exchanging leaning on Adam for leaning on Charlie?

She and Charlie planned an indefinite-date picnic for May. They invited people to the farm for the first weekend in May when the temperature was over seventy degrees. The party was Charlie's idea but Michelle went along with it enthusiastically. They laid in supplies ahead of time and when the first of May turned out to be very warm, they were ready for the picnic.

At eight-thirty on May first, Charlie called her with glee in his voice. "This is it. This is May Day."

Michelle looked out the window at the blue sky. There were no clouds and the day looked gorgeous. "Are you sure it's going to be over seventy?" she asked.

"The weather forecast is for 80 degrees," he answered. "I heard it on the news. You call Tim and Tracy and Doreen. Have them call everyone else. I'll pick you up at ten. Okay?"

Michelle said yes and ran to her room to get dressed for the big day. She'd looked forward to spring with such longing. Wisconsin winters seemed to drag on and on. But the summer was really coming and they were going to greet it with the biggest, happiest party of all. She was glad that Charlie liked to give parties so much. It made life fun.

Dressing in her bright green cotton shirt, her pink cardigan sweater and her lime green cotton slacks, Michelle was singing a happy song as she brushed her hair. Her outfit made her look cheerful, Michelle decided, and she smiled at the reflection she saw in the mirror. Life was good and she was happy.

By ten o'clock, Michelle was standing on the porch, waiting for Charlie, who waved as he drove up in his beat-up old Porsche. He looked as happy and excited as she was and he kissed her as she climbed into the car. His first words were, "Susie not coming?"

"She's coming later with Tim." Michelle stuck her hand out the rolled-down window and let the warm air brush against her fingers. "It's really here, isn't it?" she asked. Then she remembered that today was Sunday and she hadn't called Adam. For a moment, guilt threatened to drown her joy. How could she have forgotten Adam, just because she was excited about a sunny day?

She glanced at her watch. It was ten-fifteen. If she didn't do something fast, they would be at the farm and there was no telephone there. She asked, "Would you mind stopping for a Coke? I want to make a phone call."

"Sure," Charlie said. Was that tightening around his mouth a sign that he knew who she was going to call? Michelle wasn't sure and she didn't dare say anything more. Her happy mood was turning blue around the edges. Nervously she twisted the ring on her finger.

When he pulled into the diner, she said, "Order me a Coke, will you? I'll be right back."

It was easy enough to transfer the charges from the pay phone to her home. Adam answered the telephone, even though it was before their usual time of eleven. She said, "I'm on my way to a party, so I called early."

"How are things?" Adam asked.

"Good," Michelle answered. Again, she felt a lump of guilt lodge in her throat. She had been so happy earlier. Happier than she'd ever imagined she could be without Adam. "It's a real nice day. Over seventy five. We're having a party to celebrate summer."

"You and Charlie?" Adam asked. There was no malice in his voice, only a bit of sadness.

"Yes," Michelle answered. She waited for him to say more. Why didn't he object?

But Adam talked only of the weather, telling her it was almost ninety there. Michelle said, "I guess our seventy degrees seems like small stuff to you."

"I wish I were there," Adam said. This time there was a fierceness in his voice that made Michelle know he was telling the truth. "I miss you, Mitchy. I love you."

The operator broke in and said their three minutes were up. Michelle was happy because it gave her a chance to duck the implied question in Adam's declaration of love. She said good-bye and hung up, promising to call again next Sunday. He said, "Have a great time." Then he added, "Say hello to Charlie," and hung up.

Michelle slipped into the booth beside

Charlie, trying desperately to recapture her happy mood. She said, "I'll drink this fast, I promise."

"How's Adam?" Charlie asked.

"He said to say hello," Michelle answered. "He's all right."

"I guess he misses you a lot?"

"I guess so."

"Aren't you sure?" Charlie asked.

Michelle looked at him and sighed. "Charlie, I don't know what to say about me and Adam. We still talk on the telephone a lot. We still write and I guess we're still . . . close. But I don't know what else to tell you."

Charlie closed his hand over hers. She was uncomfortably aware that his warm touch was covering Adam's ring. He said, "Tell me to mind my own business. You'll figure it out in time, Michelle."

Michelle smiled at him and said, "You're a nice person, Charlie. Did anyone ever tell you that?"

"And you're holding up the best party in the world with that Coke," Charlie said. "Drink up and let's go."

As they walked to the car, Michelle wondered if it wouldn't be easier for her if either Charlie or Adam gave her an ultimatum. One or the other of them might insist that she make up her mind, and choose between them. Surely, both Adam and Charlie were capable of such an ultimatum. She drifted into a daydream where both boys were standing in front of her, insisting that

144

she choose. But when she tried to choose, her daydreams disintegrated into worried fragments. She wasn't ready.

The party, like all of Charlie's parties, was a success. There were more kids than they'd invited but the extras weren't too rowdy and the old farmhouse wasn't fancy enough to worry about. Kids brought some of their own food and drinks even though Charlie and Michelle provided hot dogs, sandwiches, baked beans, and potato chips. They'd made the beans two weeks earlier and frozen them. Michelle tried to light the oven of the old stove in the dilapidated kitchen but after ten minutes, they decided to simply heat the beans on top of the stove. "Not the best I've ever done," Michelle said ruefully, as she surveyed the thawing beans sitting in the heavy black skillet.

"You're a wonderful cook," Charlie assured her and kissed her on the cheek. "Will you marry me?"

Michelle laughed and drew away quickly. "Wait till you taste my chocolate covered snails," she teased. "Or my French fried spider legs."

By two-thirty, the farmhouse was overflowing with kids who were sitting around on the floor, listening to music and talking. Michelle tried to get them outdoors into the sunshine, but most of them seemed quite comfortable in the house. One explained, "It's cozy here."

"Closer to the refrigerator," said another, more honestly.

Michelle shook her head in mock dismay and said to Charlie, "Well, I'm going outside on this first summer day. Come with me?"

They walked hand in hand past the pond, over the little hill and onto the flat meadow beyond. Charlie held her hand and pointed out how far his land boundaries were. "Forty-five tillable acres," he said proudly. "And another thirty of forest. Want to see?"

"All seventy-five acres?" Michelle asked. "I didn't wear my hiking shoes."

"We can walk over to the woods," Charlie offered. "The fields are dry. I was there the other day."

Michelle looked down at her white sandals. Despite what Charlie said, the ground was far from dry and her shoes were already covered with black mud. The bottoms of her light green pants were getting wet from brushing against the new grass. She nodded in agreement and followed Charlie across his meadow toward the forest lands.

As they walked, Charlie talked of the future on his farm. "I called a guy yesterday about renting out the fields. My dad never thought it was worth the effort, but I think this guy will pay me eight dollars an acre. That's about four hundred dollars. If I get someone to thin the forest, they'll pay me for the wood they take out. Maybe pick up another six hundred. That's over a thousand. Next year, I figure I can use that money to rent the tractor and equipment I need and work my own fields."

"You're really serious about this farming thing, aren't you?" Michelle asked. It still seemed odd to her to think of Charlie on a tractor.

"I'm serious," Charlie said. "I figure if I work real hard, I'll have a real farm by the time you get out of college." He stopped, apparently afraid he'd betrayed too much of his dream.

Michelle begged, "I don't want you to plan your life around me."

He turned to face her, smiling as he said, "But you can't stop me from dreaming, can you?" Then he said, laughing, "If I see you as a captive princess in my ivory tower, what's wrong with that? You might learn to love it there."

She looked up at the tall boy in front of her. The warm sun was beating down on them and the sunshine framed his dark blond straight hair with a kind of halo. Though not handsome, his blue eyes were beautiful and Michelle felt her heart melt as she looked into them. Charlie was so good, so honest, and so sweet. One more time, she tried to find the words she needed to tell him the truth. "I like you, Charlie. I've had a wonderful time with you these last few weeks, but I . . ."

"But you don't love me," Charlie finished for her. He put on a deep theatrical voice and waved his arm dramatically, as he said, "But,

Lucinda, you must realize, I have enough love for both of us."

"Don't turn this away with a joke," Michelle said. She hurt for him, but she felt she had to make him understand. "I like you a lot," she repeated. "But I'm not sure of anything else. . . ." She faltered, partly out of concern for him and partly because she didn't want to lose him. She would hate to lose Charlie. Losing Adam was enough.

He took her hand again and said seriously, "I want to farm for myself. It's the one thing I've ever really wanted in this world." Then he grinned and added, "I don't think of you as a *thing*."

Suddenly, Michelle remembered yesterday evening at her home. She saw the way her mother and father sat in front of the television, eating popcorn, watching a TV movie, and joking during the commercials. So much of their time together seemed sort of ordinary and dull but they were so happy to be living the life they were living. Last night, her father had rumpled Michelle and Susie's hair and said, "You girls are getting to be pretty. Almost as pretty as your mother."

And she'd looked at her husband with that pleased, *don't-be-silly* expression. All she'd said was, "You must be getting blind in your old age," but there had been pride in her words. Pride and love.

Will I ever have that kind of secure love? Michelle asked herself. *I thought I had it once with Adam. Will I ever have it again? Could I have it with Charlie?*

For the rest of the walk, Charlie talked about his plans for farming, about his father's opposition to those plans and about his determination to follow his own ambitions. He said, "I don't know why parents are always so sure they know what is best for you. I mean, why should my father be so sure that farming is wrong and sales is right? Just because he's in sales."

Michelle thought of Adam and his struggles with Charlotte. She was also sure she knew what was best for her son, insisting that being a veterinarian was not nearly as good an idea as becoming a professor of literature. "Maybe your father wants you to be a better salesman than he is," Michelle said.

"Your folks never bug you, do they?" Charlie asked as he nodded his head in agreement.

"My folks want me to be happy and healthy," Michelle said. Then she grinned. "And they think teaching is a great idea. If I said I wanted to join the circus, I imagine they'd start screaming." She thought of how strongly they'd pushed her into dating after Adam left town. But they'd chosen not to push further when she'd settled for Charlie, even though they would prefer that she be dating many fellows as Susie was doing.

"My folks try to let me do what I want," Michelle said. "When I know what I want," she added ruefully.

Twelve

May was a warm and beautiful month. The skies were uninterruptedly blue and the land bloomed so quickly that Michelle felt as though the whole month was a burst of flowers. Before she adjusted to the soft, clear springtime, June arrived and the days stretched into the warmer, fuller summertime.

School became a waste of time and even good students like Michelle spent hours staring out the window at the beautiful green countryside. She lived for three o'clock when everyone was let out into the golden day. The precious daylight hours between three and seven seemed all too short; Michelle longed for weekends and dreamed of summer vacation.

She and Charlie spent a lot of time at his farm, walking over the fields, watching the farmer he'd rented his land to plow the dark, heavy earth. On mild days, they took a picnic and sat at the edge of the pond, scattering crumbs for the birds and watching their reflections in the water. Michelle began to love the old farm almost as much as Charlie did and when he talked of their future there, she seldom corrected his dreams. Was it wrong to dream, she asked herself, and let the truth slip away on a summer's cloud.

Adam changed his hours at the supermarket on May fourth and he was now working almost full time. When his school was out, on June seventh, he would begin a forty-four hour week. Because he was often working on Sunday mornings now, there was no special time to call him. Michelle missed talking to Adam on Sundays, and hated the knowledge that they were drifting farther and farther apart, but they'd found no solution to their dilemma.

Adam called her when he could, sometimes reversing the charges. He usually aimed for her dinner hour, knowing the Karlsens were strict about everyone showing up for that meal. So they talked, perhaps as often as always, but the familiarity of a regular hour was missing. Michelle tried not to mind the fact that she must wait for Adam to call her these days, just as she tried not to mind the terrible knowledge that Adam would not be visiting this summer. She tried to accept the inevitable and drift with the luscious summer days.

She sat on the fresh, green grass in front of Charlie's pond, with her back against a tree stump, her legs curled under her body, and tossed pebbles into the water. Charlie sat beside her, drinking a Pepsi and talking about his plans for the future. "We really should get that stuff out of the attic tomorrow," he said in a worried voice.

"If it's not too hot," Michelle agreed.

"If we clean it all up this week, take the clothes to the laundromat, and sort the music sheets, then we can drive to Madison next Saturday. There's a lot of antique stores there; I checked the yellow pages."

Michelle yawned and stretched her legs out in front of her. She was wearing white shorts and she noted that her olive skin was turning to a golden brown. She would have a good tan before school was out at the end of June. "We can't go to Madison next Saturday," she reminded him. "It's the prom."

"The prom? Already?" Charlie asked.

"Silly," laughed Michelle. "Today is the seventh of June. School will be out in two and a half weeks." As she said the words aloud, a lump formed in her throat. Today was the seventh, the last day of school for Adam. His summer vacation had officially begun an hour ago. At the painful realization, the lump moved from her throat down into her chest. She quickly turned her mind to other things. "I promised we'd work at the refreshment stand for an hour. From eleven to twelve, okay?"

"Okay."

Charlie never argued with her. If it had been Adam, he might have objected, saying he wanted to leave the dance before then, or that he didn't want to work on his prom night. But that wasn't really fair, was it? Adam had been generous about doing things for other people. No need to twist her memories in an attempt to keep from missing him so much.

She stood up and said, "I want to take a walk."

"Okay," Charlie said, and got to his feet.

Michelle wanted to tell Charlie to stay behind, that she had meant she wanted to walk alone, but she didn't. It wasn't fair to Charlie to shut him out just because she was thinking of Adam. Besides, Charlie was her boyfriend now — or at least everyone thought he was. Sometimes she wondered what Charlie thought about Adam and her. He never asked.

They headed toward the forested land, skirting the newly plowed fields. Holding hands, they walked quietly, each bound in his own thoughts. Michelle was pretty sure that Charlie was thinking about his future on the farm; his interest in farming was growing stronger each day. She was trying to think of anything at all except how much she missed Adam. The very idea of going to the prom with anyone but Adam seemed horrible. For as long as she could remember, she and Adam had gone to formal dances together.

"Penny for your thoughts," Charlie said.

"No thoughts," Michelle said quickly.

"Heard from Adam lately?"

"Nothing new," Michelle answered. Charlie must have known she was thinking of Adam. Well, she couldn't help that. She couldn't help thinking what she was thinking.

"Michelle," Charlie began, "I've been thinking about Adam and you. Maybe you ought to try and go to California this summer. You know, maybe if you saw him, you'd find out that things have changed." Then he added, "Or not changed."

"My folks won't let me go to California," Michelle said dully. "Besides, I don't have the money."

"It's not so expensive," Charlie said. "There are budget fares from Chicago for a hundred dollars each way. That's just two hundred and twenty something with tax. I could loan you the money."

Michelle stopped and looked at Charlie. She reached up and touched his cheek and said, "You know something, Charlie Johnson? You're sweet."

Charlie grinned and nodded his head. "And you can pay the money back whenever you want. No interest. No strings."

She shook her head. "They wouldn't let me. I know they wouldn't let me."

"Have you asked?"

"Yes," she said, and then she remembered that the last time she'd asked had been last January when she'd been so desperate. Now that she was recovered from that despair, they might reconsider their attitude. Was it possible? Slowly, she said, "I might ask again. But are you sure . . ."

"I want you to be happy, Michelle," Charlie said softly. "You've made me happy these last weeks. I want to make you happy."

"You sound like a character in an old movie," Michelle said. "Very noble."

But Charlie didn't laugh or joke. He just took her hand again and bent to kiss her cheek. He said, "I meant what I said. You should be happy."

Charlie drove her home in time for supper and they agreed to meet early the next morning to sort out the clothes and things in his attic. When they got to her door, he took her hand and said, "I don't need the money until next year, Michelle. You could baby-sit and pay it back."

"I'll talk to them," Michelle said. "And thank you."

He looked very serious as he said, "You know, of course, that I'm not totally noble in this offer. There's always the hope that you'll find out I'm your Prince Charming in disguise. Frogs often finish first, I'm told."

She laughed and hugged him, kissing him on the cheek as she said, "Oh, Charlie, you're not a frog. You're a wonderful person. And I love you."

He kissed her on the lips, holding her close and hugging her tight. As always when they kissed, Michelle felt warm and safe, but he didn't thrill her the way Adam had. She tried to respond to his kiss and when he pulled away, she smiled at him once again, saying, "I'll see you tomorrow."

"I love you," Charlie said.

Michelle got out of the car quickly and went into her house. She was somewhat shaken by Charlie's offer to lend her money and she was excited by the possibility. Her folks would probably say no, but it was worth a try.

Supper was on the table when Michelle came into the house and Susie was busy bringing in the soup. She said, "I'm glad you got home in time to eat. It was your turn tonight, you know."

"I'm sorry," Michelle said automatically. She was too excited to really be sorry but she offered, "I'll do the dishes and set the table for two nights in a row."

Susie nodded her head in cheerful acceptance of Michelle's attempt to make amends and they all sat down to eat. They talked of school's ending, of the new construction at the outskirts of town and of her mother's most troubled student before Michelle worked up the nerve to mention California. She began obliquely, "Adam got out of school today."

"School's out early in California," her mother said noncommitally.

"I was thinking I might go to visit him this summer," Michelle said quietly.

For a moment, there was no reaction at all.

Her mother looked at her father and her father looked at her mother. They seemed to be sending silent signals and finally, her mother cleared her throat and said, "Well, that's an interesting idea, but I don't think it would work."

"Why not?" Michelle's words flared, though she had promised herself she would keep cool.

"The money, for one thing," her father said.

"It's not much," she argued, "only two hundred and twenty dollars round trip from Chicago. And I could stay with them. Charlotte would be there," she added.

"You don't have two hundred and twenty dollars," her mother pointed out.

"I could borrow the money," Michelle said. "And I could pay it back later."

"Borrow?" her father asked. "Do you expect us to lend you more money?" His voice was a mix between outrage, amusement, and pity.

"A friend," Michelle explained. "A friend will loan me the money."

Her mother shook her head. "That poor boy. He's silly about you. Michelle, I wish you'd consider whether or not you're really being fair to Charlie. He's such a nice kid."

"Charlie's older than I am," she said defensively. "He's not a kid."

"You cannot borrow money from Charlie to visit Adam," her father said. It was a flat, final, and complete refusal.

Michelle wasn't surprised; she hadn't had much hope anyway. Her first reaction was regret that she'd brought the subject up. Her second reaction was anger that her folks were so strict. But most of all, she just felt a dull pain as she thought of a long, flat summer without Adam.

"What's more," her mother said, "I want you to promise us that you'll start dating other boys. Boys you might *really* like."

"You're not being fair," Michelle said.

"It's you who isn't being fair," her mother retorted. "Charlie is crazy about you and you're just leading him on."

"I'm not leading him on," Michelle protested. "You make me sound like a really terrible person."

"You're being terrible to Charlie," her mother said. "Every time I see the way he looks at you, I feel so sorry for him."

Michelle had no answer. Anything she said would just make things worse so she said nothing. Susie jumped into the void and delivered a monologue about her plans for the summer vacation. As her younger sister chattered, Michelle was grateful that Susie was trying to help unstick a difficult situation. She thanked Susie for her help after supper, saying, "You tried to smooth things over, I know. I wish Mom didn't see Charlie as a tragic figure."

Susie giggled and nodded her head in agreement, adding, "I have the feeling that Charlie will survive. He's one of those guys that women will always feel sorry for and take care of. You know, kind of cuddly and cute."

Michelle was a little surprised at Susie's assessment of Charlie. She had never thought of him as exactly cuddly before. She said, rather lamely, "Charlie's a nice person."

"He's more than that," Susie said. "He's cute. A lot of girls at school think so."

Susie's vision of Charlie helped to balance her mother's troubling insistence that she was breaking Charlie's heart. Somewhat relieved, yet still defensive, she said to Susie, "I've been honest with Charlie. He knows I'm still in love with Adam."

"Are you?" Susie asked. She raised one eyebrow as though she were privy to some special knowledge.

"Yes," Michelle said simply.

"You don't talk about him much anymore," Susie said. "Most of the time you talk about Charlie."

"That's because I'm spending so much time with him," Michelle explained.

"I wish Adam would come out," Susie said. "I miss him, too."

Michelle was touched by the idea that her sister also missed Adam, but she didn't want to talk about him any longer. She had long ago learned that talking about Adam made the pain worse. The best thing she could do was to keep busy and not think about him any more often than she had to.

"I'm going to help Charlie clean out the

attic tomorrow," she said. "Want to come along and help?"

"Have a date with Dennis," Susie answered.

"Dennis?"

"He's the new boy in my class," she explained. "He came from Chicago."

Michelle shook her head in mock dismay, but before she could say anything, the telephone rang and her mother called up, "Michelle, it's Adam."

Surprised that he was calling her at this hour, she picked up the telephone with some alarm. Her first words were, "Anything wrong?"

"Something's right," he said. "Mitchy, I'm coming out."

"Out here?"

"I'll be there on Wednesday," he said.

"How?"

"Flying to Chicago and taking the bus. The bus arrives at 7:30 Wednesday night. Will you meet me?"

"How did you . . . yes, of course . . . how did you manage?"

"I have a job in Madison," he explained. "I'll be staying with a friend of my father's in Richland Center. Michelle, it isn't La Crosse, but it's closer. We can see each other once a week. Maybe more."

"All summer?"

"Yes," Adam said, laughing. "I'll work in his supermarket as a cashier and pay him board. I wrote to him two months ago, but I didn't want to get your hopes up. This way, I'll have the money and I'll get to see you. Besides, he'll probably give me a job when we're in college next year. Aren't you glad, Mitchy? You haven't said anything."

Her breath was ragged as her body reacted to the wonderful news. Every cell, every nerve, every muscle was singing the song. "Adam is coming home!" The idea of having Adam return felt like the broken half of herself mending. She caught her breath and said softly, "Oh, Adam, you'll never know how glad."

"I think I know," Adam said. "I've missed you so much. Like bread without butter."

"Or apples without cheese," she teased. When they'd been kids, they'd always packed lunches to take to the top of the big tree in Adam's yard. Usually, those lunches had been hunks of cheese, apples, and bread and butter sandwiches. Even though they were only sixteen, they had a history behind them. How could she have ever thought that Charlie could replace Adam?

"Oh, Adam," she said. "Charlie's supposed to take me to the prom. What will I tell him?"

"Talk it over with him," Adam said. "I know this is sudden."

"I'll just tell him the truth," she decided. "I'll see if he wants to try to find another girl."

"Okay," Adam said. "It's up to you. He's been a good friend to you — to both of us."

Michelle didn't argue with Adam. One

prom seemed silly compared to the fact that Adam was coming home for the summer. That wonderful news blotted out any problems or disappointments that Charlie or anyone else might face. For the moment, she just wanted to laugh and talk to Adam, who was truly coming home!

"I'm glad," she said once again. "Oh, Adam, I'm so glad." But when she hung up the telephone, she was thinking about Charlie. What would she tell him?

Thirteen

"You'll have to go to the dance with him," her mother said. "There's no way you can back out now. Poor Charlie."

This time, instead of resenting her mother's pity for Charlie, she bowed her head in humble agreement. She was sure that Charlie would be heartbroken about Adam coming back, but there was no way around that. She would have to try and make him understand.

"I'm not sure going to the prom with him is the best idea," she said. "But he's the one that should decide — and me."

"No," her mother said firmly.

"Mother, do you really like Charlie better than Adam?"

"That has nothing to do with it," her father broke in. "And you know it. We like Adam, but we don't want you to break your promise to Charlie or anyone else. Talk to Charlie, if you have to. But *you* won't break the date. Understood?"

"Understood," Michelle said quietly. Maybe her folks were right. Maybe she really did owe it to Charlie to go to the dance with him, even though the thought of dating someone else when Adam was in town was very hard. It was Adam she loved.

She stood up, said, "I guess that's it. I'll tell Charlie about Adam when he gets here. If he wants to, I'll still go to the prom with him, all right?"

Her parents nodded their heads in agreement, then her mother patted Michelle's two clenched hands that were resting on top of the table. "It will work out, dear."

Michelle nodded her head, and took a deep breath to prepare for the scene she would soon have with Charlie. How would he take it? It was hard to imagine that Charlie would ever be really angry with her, but he would have a right to be, wouldn't he? She'd as much as told him that Adam would be in California for the summer. Still, she was pretty sure that Charlie would accept the news quietly. She just hoped it didn't hurt him too much.

When Charlie came for her, she took his hand and said, "Let's just drive out to the river for a minute. I have something I want to tell you."

He glanced sharply at her and then nodded his head. They drove in silence until they parked beside the boat docks. "There's a lot of boats already in the water," she began. "Summer's really here."

"Yes."

"Charlie, you know I told you that Adam wouldn't be coming out this summer?"

"And he is?"

She nodded her head. That much, at least, had been easy. She turned to look at Charlie and said with tears in her eyes, "We can still be friends. And I'll still go to the prom with you, if you want."

"When does he get here?" Charlie asked. There was a quiet defeat in his voice. She wanted to reach out and hold him, as she would a child that needed comforting. Even as she was feeling this, she realized that many of her feelings for Charlie were of friendship rather than of romantic love.

She took his hand and stroked it with her other hand. "He's coming on Wednesday night. I'm meeting him at the bus station."

"All summer?"

"He's working in Madison," Michelle explained. Then she went on to tell him how he had arranged it and how happy they both were that things had worked out so they could see each other at least once a week.

"How about me?" Charlie asked.

That was the question she had been waiting for — the question she had dreaded. "It's Adam I love," she said. "I wasn't sure until I heard he was coming home. It's like a lot of my emotions were underground. But when I heard he was coming and felt how happy I was, I knew that nothing had really changed between Adam and me. I guess it's always been Adam."

There was no response. Charlie started the car and drove her back to the house. When they got there, she asked, "Do you want to come in? Have a Coke or something?"

"Nope," Charlie answered. "I'm going out to the farm for a while."

There was no sense pretending that things weren't changed between them. Things were very changed. She touched Charlie's hand once again and whispered, "I'm sorry."

Charlie nodded and looked straight ahead. He was obviously waiting for her to get out of the car. Seeing that there was nothing else to do, she obliged. Once out, she turned and said again, "I'm sorry."

Charlie nodded and answered, "You couldn't help it."

Tears blinded Michelle as she walked into her house. She went directly to her room, avoiding the kitchen and the curious faces of her family. She didn't want to hear her mother say, "Poor Charlie," ever again. Once in her room, she decided to spend the day going through her closets and sorting out her dresser drawers. She needed something simple to keep her occupied while she waited for Adam's arrival. It was much later that she realized that, in a way, she was keeping her promise to Charlie to clean out *his* attic.

That evening, she stayed home with her

parents and watched television. On Sunday, she went to church with her mother and then to the movies with Susie. The next two days, she studied for her final exams, which were all on Wednesday morning. *Just as well,* Michelle told herself, *keeps me from worrying.*

But the truth was that she was worried — very worried. What if Adam had changed? What if her feelings toward Adam had changed? What if . . . The thoughts rolled round and round in her head during every unoccupied moment. Most of the thoughts were about Adam but some of them were about Charlie. Had she made a mistake in telling Charlie she would go to the prom with him? And was it really the best thing for Charlie? He was obviously very upset.

She saw Charlie in English every day. He nodded and didn't smile. Once, during a study period, she'd looked up from her book and seen his gaze on her. There was such raw pain, such longing, that she'd shivered in shame. Charlie was very, very unhappy and it was her fault.

On Wednesday morning, she'd whispered, "Good luck," as they went into class to face the final examination together. She'd smiled and hoped her eyes conveyed the genuine concern she had for him. He'd returned her smile briefly and also returned the greeting, "Good luck." She wasn't sure whether he'd meant on the exam or because she was meeting Adam that evening.

She breezed through her three exams,

barely bothering to be nervous about them, she was so nervous about seeing Adam again after all this time. What would he look like? Would he have changed? She worried that he would find her changed — perhaps not as pretty as the California girls. Yet, her good sense told her that he'd gone through a lot of trouble and difficulty to get back to Wisconsin to be with her. Adam would be just as loving as always. If anything, she was the one who might have changed.

She was early and the bus was late. As more time elapsed, Michelle convinced herself she wouldn't recognize Adam, or that he would decide upon first sight that he no longer loved her. She paced up and down the sidewalk in front of the bus station, hating herself for being so silly and knowing that if the bus didn't get here soon, she would die from anticipation.

Twenty minutes after it was due, the Greyhound bus rolled into the station. Michelle stood beside the door, holding her breath as she watched passengers disembark. First, came an old lady with a cane. After that, a tired-looking woman with three children got off. Then, two other older people and a middle-aged couple got off the bus. Michelle waited, watching to see if other passengers would get off, and a part of her was sure that Adam would not be among them. It was almost as though she'd waited so long and hoped so hard, that it couldn't be true that he had really arrived.

But there he was, looking exactly like Adam. He might have been gone only a week or two, he was so unchanged. He was even wearing the Levi jacket he'd worn the day she'd put him and Charlotte on the airplane. His greeting was as normal and unemotional as he looked. "Hi, Mitchy. Great to see you."

Then she was in his arms, holding him tight and being held tighter as the tears ran down her cheeks. "Oh, Adam, I missed you. You'll never know how I missed you."

His arms gripped her and his words came carefully as he said, "I think I can guess. I missed you, too." He kissed away the tears and laughed as he grabbed her around the waist and said, "Hey, I'm hungry. How about a cheeseburger at the Bodega? I've missed that almost as much as I've missed you."

"My folks are expecting you for supper," Michelle said. "And later, I told Bert we'd come over. A bunch of kids want to say hello."

Adam frowned and Michelle's heart caught as she realized he wasn't pleased by her arrangements. Adam had never liked large groups of people and he'd probably planned on being alone with her tonight. "When I called Bert to see if you could stay there," she explained, "he sort of took over."

"Sure," Adam said and smiled at her.

She felt the old surge of excitement as she basked in Adam's smile. He'd always had the most beautiful smile in the world and now that she'd not seen him for several months, she was struck by how handsome he was.

169

Had Adam always been that handsome? Probably. But seeing him tonight was almost like seeing him for the first time. "I feel shy," she confessed.

He nodded and squeezed her waist. "That's natural," he said. "But the time apart has done you a lot of good."

"Why?"

"You're more beautiful than ever," he teased. "So beautiful, I can hardly stand to look at you. I'm dazzled."

She laughed and said, "I feel the same way about you. Really."

He caught her to him again and kissed her. She felt herself responding with all the old fervor and something new — an excitement that had never been there before. As she kissed him, she felt as though the ground was not solid under her feet. She wanted to cry out to him, "Hold me, Adam. Hold me and never let me go."

Eventually, he did let her go and asked, "Do we really have to go to Bert's? Can't we just go down to the river and neck?"

She laughed and pulled away, saying in the old teasing tone, "Down boy. Down. Besides, it was all I could do to keep them from all coming down to the bus station with me. Susie, too."

"Susie," Adam said and he smiled again. "How's Susie?"

His smile was like sunshine, Michelle decided. It warmed the whole world. She leaned her head against his chest and said, "She's fine. In love with a different boy each week."

The driver had put all the luggage out on the sidewalk now. Adam picked his up with his left hand, keeping his right arm firmly around Michelle's waist. As they started walking toward the car, he picked up the conversation, saying, "So, little Susie's in love."

"With a different boy each week," Michelle repeated.

"I'm glad I got the sensible sister."

A sharp pain hit Michelle as she thought about Charlie. She didn't feel very sensible about the way she'd treated him. Now that Adam was here beside her, she wished she'd never dated Charlie. It would have been better if she'd been faithful as they promised each other. She felt as if, somehow, she'd failed Adam.

But they were together now and that was all that mattered. Adam said he would stay in La Crosse until next Sunday. He would report to work in Madison on Monday morning. "I was really lucky to get the job," he said. "And the best part is that Sam's house is in Richland Center. That's only two hours away from La Crosse. Of course, the supermarket is way out on the outskirts of Madison. Only a half hour from Sam's house. So it worked out perfectly. What if he lived on the other side of Madison? It would be almost four hours from you."

"Two hours isn't so far," Michelle said. Privately, she worried about how often her folks would let her have the car to drive to

Richland Center. Most of their dates would probably have to be by bus. But there wouldn't be all that much time for dates anyway. Adam would be working as many hours as he could.

"He said he could give me at least forty," Adam continued. "Maybe more. The trouble is if I get over forty-eight hours a week, they have to pay me time and a half. I wanted to duck out of that — I'd work more if I could — but the union says no dice."

"I'm glad you can't work any more," Michelle said. "If you did, I'd never see you."

"I'll need the money," Adam reminded her. "Charlotte still won't budge about tuition for Wisconsin."

"How is Charlotte?" Michelle asked. She tried to keep any bitterness she felt out of her voice.

"Mom's fine. She's got some friends now. Even dating some guy who teaches literature at her college. I think she may go back to school herself nights and get her degree.

"That's wonderful," Michelle said. Privately, she thought that if Charlotte found someone else to love, she might loosen up a bit on Adam. "You two getting along better?"

"We were until I pulled this on her," Adam said. His voice betrayed his joy at being in Wisconsin and the pain he felt at displeasing his mother once again. "I presented the whole plan to her as a package and there really wasn't much she could do. Poor Charlotte, she loves me so much and she doesn't know how to show it."

He's changed, Michelle thought. In the old days, he didn't recognize his mother's love or her need to hold on to him. And there were other little changes that she recognized — a new seriousness, a preoccupation with the future. Beside Adam, she felt young and somehow frivolous. The thought repeated itself — *he's changed.*

But no one else seemed to see any changes at all in Adam. Each person they met said in a surprised voice, or a happy one, "You haven't changed a bit."

By the time supper with her family was over, Michelle had forgotten her initial fears that things would be different between Adam and her. It was so easy to slip back into the wonderful warm feelings of togetherness that they'd held for so many years. She had no doubt that Adam was feeling the same way about her because each time she looked at him, his eyes returned her gaze with a loving message. No matter how much Adam had changed, his love toward her was the same, Michelle decided. That was all that was really important, wasn't it?

The kids at Bert's had gathered by the time she and Adam arrived. There were a lot of them; at least thirty dropped in during the evening. Michelle wondered if Adam noticed that Charlie was not one of the guests. *Later*, she told herself, *later will be time to talk about Charlie.* She sat beside Adam, holding his hand and smiling as he talked and laughed with his other friends.

Two or three times someone slipped and said, "Michelle and Charlie," as they talked about the events of last winter. If Adam minded, he didn't show it. Once, Tracy said, "And when Charlie gave Michelle the birthday party . . ." then she clapped her hand over her mouth and looked at Michelle. "I'm sorry," she whispered.

"Adam knows about that party," Michelle said stiffly.

"Nothing to worry about," Adam said and then he added, "I wouldn't want Michelle to stay home in the corner all winter and turn into a grump, you know."

"How about the girls in California?" Tim Hardin asked. "Are they all beautiful?"

"A lot are," Adam admitted.

"Did you date any movie stars?" Tim persisted.

"I dated a model," Adam said, and then he squeezed Michelle's hand and added, "Of course, she wasn't nearly as pretty as any of the girls in La Crosse. Best-looking girls in the world."

The conversation moved on to basketball and Michelle was glad because she'd found Adam's confession about dating someone else too painful. She certainly didn't want to hear about any more girls. Still, she knew that Adam had wanted to be reassuring when he said that about La Crosse girls. And what right did she have to be jealous?

On the way home, she said, "I have to talk to you about Charlie."

"You don't have to," Adam replied.

"I want to," Michelle said. "I know you knew I was dating him, but I'm not sure you know everything. I was sort of going steady with Charlie." She waited for his response.

There was a long silence and then Adam asked, "How did that happen?" The coolness in his voice frightened her.

"I was lonely," Michelle said quickly. "And I thought you were never coming back. I was afraid I'd lost you."

She wanted to lean against him, to have him comfort her and to tell her that everything was all right. Instead, he asked, "But how about Charlie? You must have liked him a lot to say you'd go steady with him."

"I never felt about Charlie the way I feel about you. He was just sort of there." She felt that her explanation was lame, but it was as close to the truth as she could come. When the silence became too prolonged, she added, "You dated girls."

"Yes," Adam said. "But I didn't go steady. I didn't even date one particular girl. Mitchy, I knew you were seeing a lot of Charlie, but I never guessed it was serious."

"It wasn't serious," Michelle protested. The lump in her throat competed with the knots in her stomach for attention. She wished she'd never told Adam about Charlie.

Finally, Adam asked, "Are you sure, Mitchy? Really sure?"

"Yes."

"Poor Charlie."

Michelle managed a tiny little laugh. "You sound like my mother."

But Adam didn't respond. He stared out at the black night and she felt fear filling the car. What was he thinking? Finally, she said, "You've changed. You're more serious."

"I knew when I left that you'd date other guys," Adam said, as he stared out at the darkness. His voice was troubled and low. "I figured that it would be good for you to experiment a little, see what the world had to offer. I didn't think that we were risking much, Mitchy. What we had was so special."

She caught her breath at his use of the word *had*. Why was Adam using the past tense?

"But it never occurred to me you'd find one guy and stick with him. I don't know what to think. Either you had something important going with Charlie or you were using him."

"That's not fair!" Michelle cried. "I was lonely!"

"So was I."

"You're the one who left," Michelle accused. The surprising anger boiled up and she thought that she had changed, too. Until Adam left, she'd never known about her capacity for anger. She'd never known how strong and immediate her reactions could be.

"That's not fair," Adam said. He was angry now, too. "You know I had no choice."

"You had choices," Michelle protested, but

176

she knew they had not been real ones. She conceded, "I guess you did the best you could. But you did leave me," she added. "And usually, I was the one who had to call you."

"Is that why you had to have Charlie?" Adam asked bitterly. "Did you have to have someone else following you around?"

"Oh!" Michelle cried. "That is really not fair!"

But his words stayed in her head, and she knew she had to learn to stand alone.

Suddenly, the argument collapsed around them. Adam pulled her closer to him, burying his face in her hair and saying, "I missed you so much, Michelle. I guess I'm jealous."

Michelle let her head relax against his shoulder. She was filled with joy and love, and a new understanding of herself. Adam was home again. They were together again. She snuggled closer to him and said, "I was jealous, too. But you're here now."

Their kiss was long and soft, a gentle homecoming. Michelle felt as though the whole car was a golden circle of love. Waves of happiness washed through her, and the prospect of having Adam by her side this summer was so delicious that she sighed as she laid her head on his shoulder.

Later, much later, she said gently, "I have to go to the prom with him. I promised."

"Poor Charlie," Adam said. "You owe him an apology. Maybe I do, too. I guess we'd both better go talk to him tomorrow."

"No," Michelle said quickly. "I'll go alone."

Fourteen

Charlie didn't seem surprised when she called him and asked if she could come over. He simply suggested they meet on the steps of the public library, adding in his wry voice, "Neutral territory."

He was waiting for her when she got there and his first words were, "Adam didn't come with you?"

"I wanted to talk to you alone."

He nodded his head and asked, "Want to walk?"

They walked down the shady side of the street, letting the spots of sunlight catch them in haphazard patterns of polka dots. By the time they'd reached the edge of town, Michelle had managed to talk about exams, Adam's job, and the graduation party. Finally, she said in exasperation, "You're not very talkative, Charlie."

"I figured if I let you rattle on long enough, you'd tell me why you called me."

"I wanted to clear things up between us before the prom," Michelle said. "I wanted to apologize."

He shook his head. "Nothing to apologize about. But about the prom, I'm working on another date. I think Sally Nelsen will go with me. I heard her date had the mumps. So I called and asked Betty. Sally wasn't home but Betty said she was sure the answer would be yes."

"You're working on another date?" Michelle repeated.

Charlie nodded and grinned. "It might not feel so bad to be dumped by the prettiest girl in school if the next prettiest one is available." Then a shadow crossed his face and he said wistfully, "At least that's the theory."

Michelle didn't know what to say. Of course, she hoped that Sally would say yes and then her problem would be solved. She could go to the prom with Adam and everything would turn out just right. She asked softly, "Are you sure?"

"Nope," Charlie answered, pretending not to understand her question, and glancing at his watch. "But she should be home by now. Let's go get a Coke and I'll call her."

They went into a little variety store on the corner and Michelle sat down on one of the three stools in the place and ordered two Cokes while Charlie went to the telephone. From where she was sitting, she could see

Charlie dialing and then talking on the phone. He talked a long time and seemed to be having a great time with whoever was on the other end. Once, he even laughed out loud. Michelle was aware that she wasn't feeling all that cheerful herself. Could it be that she really had left-over feelings for Charlie? Could she be in love with both Charlie and Adam at the same time? What was wrong with her? Why couldn't she be happy if Charlie was happy?

And Charlie *was* happy when he returned. "Betty said yes. Sally still wasn't home but Betty was positive about the answer. I've got a date with Betty for the next week. She said they'd never done that before, dated the same guy, but that they were willing to try it with me. That should be a trip."

"If you start dating both the Nelsen twins, you'll be taking out the *two* prettiest girls in school," Michelle said.

He may have heard something in her voice that betrayed her dismay or he may have been just being Charlie. For whatever reason, Charlie shook his head and said, "Michelle, you're the prettiest girl in school. And the sweetest and the best. There'll never be another princess like you. But maybe that last kiss did turn me into something other than a frog after all."

"Oh Charlie!" She was laughing a little and crying a little as she twisted the straw top. Abruptly, she stood up and said, "I guess I'll get going."

180

When she reported her conversation to Adam that afternoon, she tried to tell it as matter of factly as possible, but by the time she finished, Adam was laughing at her.

"What's funny?" she demanded.

"You are," Adam teased. "You wanted to break the poor guy's heart and he's recovered too fast to suit you."

"I didn't want to break his heart!"

"No? Well, you at least wanted to bend it a little, didn't you?"

"Charlie's heart *was* broken!" she protested. "He's just going out with Betty to be nice."

"Yeah, Betty's pretty nice," Adam laughed and pulled her close to him.

Michelle laughed and pretended to push him away, saying, "I'd forgotten how awful you could be."

"You just say that because you love me," Adam said, and kissed the tip of her nose. "And because I read minds."

Michelle kissed him and then said, "It's wonderful to be with someone who understands you. Someone you don't have to explain yourself to all the time."

"Not dull?" Adam asked as he kissed the back of her neck.

"No," Michelle sighed and nestled closer in his arms. "Not dull at all."

Adam borrowed a dark jacket from Michelle's father and wore his own dark slacks to the prom. He'd tried to rent a tuxedo but they were all taken in his size. As he called for her at the door, he looked down ruefully at his mismatched suit and asked, "You sure you want to be seen with me?"

Michelle's eyes were sparkling as she reached up on tiptoes and kissed him on the cheek. She whispered, "I've never been surer about anything, Adam. Our Junior Prom and we're together again. Oh, Adam, you'll never know how I've wished and hoped for this night."

He seemed to forget all about his own discomfort at her words and smiled as he said, "Me too, Mitchy."

They double-dated with Susie and Tim Hardin, sitting in the back of the car holding hands as Tim drove his father's Lincoln up to the door of the high school gymnasium. Susie had worked all afternoon decorating the gymnasium with crepe paper streamers and artificial flowers. As secretary of the freshman class, it was her job to supervise the decorations and the selling of refreshments. She complained bitterly at being overworked, but Michelle knew she was proud of her responsibilities. When Adam learned that they were expected to work an hour at the refreshment stand, he didn't complain a bit, making Michelle realize that he really was a lot more grown-up than he used to be.

The motif of the brightly decorated dance was "Pennies From Heaven," and large copper-colored discs dropped from the high gymnasium ceiling. The artificial flowers were all in yellows and oranges to go with the copper and for the first time, Michelle understood her sister's insistence on the lime-green taffeta dress she was wearing. Spinning around on the dance floor, Susie would look like a golden nymph in a forest of earth colors. "Everything's beautiful," Michelle assured her.

"Do you really think so?" Susie asked. "I wanted it to be the very best ever for you and Adam."

Michelle took her sister's hand and squeezed it in gratitude. "It's the very best ever," she assured her. As she watched Susie drift onto the dance floor, she reminded herself that things had turned out very well this year after all. She was good friends with her sister once again. She had Adam, wonderful Adam, by her side. She was a lucky girl.

In a lot of ways, Michelle felt that she had the best of her old and new lives combined. The months without Adam had taught her a great deal. She had new friends. The future wasn't spelled out for them, but that no longer bothered her. *I'm a different Michelle,* she thought. What would happen when Adam left again? The warning pain convinced her not to think about that much. Fleetingly, she knew it wouldn't ever hurt as much as it had the first time. And she promised herself that she would try to keep her life better balanced —not all depending on a boy.

Right after she and Adam finished at the refreshment stand, Charlie asked her to dance. She'd been waiting for that, expecting it, really. All evening, she'd seen him with Sally, apparently having a wonderful time. He looked relaxed as he approached her and she found herself returning his smile as easily as if they were just old friends. Whatever feelings she'd had for Charlie had not been serious feelings. Now that she had Adam beside her, she could measure the difference between her response to the two men.

Charlie slipped his arm around her waist and asked in a soft voice, "Miss me?"

"You're having a good time, aren't you?" Michelle said, sidestepping the question.

"No," Charlie answered himself. "I guess you don't miss me yet. But I just found out that Adam's not home to stay."

"Of course not," Michelle said. "I thought you knew that."

"Nope," Charlie said, smiling. "But I know it now and I figure when he goes away again, there'll be a chance for me again. I'll wait."

"Charlie, don't do that," Michelle said sharply.

"Why not?"

"Because when Adam leaves this time, I won't be running back to you. It isn't fair to you . . . or me."

"All's fair in love and war," Charlie answered and swung her around sharply, throwing her slightly off balance so that he could catch her in his arms.

"I won't just fall back into your arms,"

Michelle said. "So don't count on that." Then she added, "Date other girls, Charlie. There are lots of girls who would like to go out with you."

"Yeah," Charlie agreed. "That's one of the things I learned by taking you out. That all these years, I've been a prince in disguise."

"You really are," Michelle said earnestly.

"So if I'm a prince and you're a princess, then we belong together. Simple, isn't it?"

She was smiling as she said, "Life isn't always like that, Charlie. Believe me, I won't be back."

"I'll wait and see," he said stubbornly. Then he grinned and added, "Of course, while I'm waiting, I think I might as well spend some time with Betty and Sally. But you just remember that my heart belongs to you."

"You'll be all right," Michelle said, and then she laughed. "In fact, you're recovering a little too fast for it to be very flattering."

"Just say the word," Charlie assured her, "and I'm yours."

"When Adam leaves this time," Michelle said seriously, "I'll date lots of different fellows. I won't stick with one guy. It isn't what I want."

"At least you admit that you'll go out with others," Charlie said. "And I'll be one of the others."

"Maybe," Michelle admitted. "But, believe me, I won't settle down into a comfortable rut, trying to duplicate what Adam and I have. I'll be on my own."

185

Charlie's face showed that he'd heard her this time. He nodded and said, "Okay, Michelle. Anyway, I want you to know it was fun."

Michelle drew his head down so that she could touch his cheek with her lips. She said softly, "It *was* fun."

Even though the music played on, their conversation was obviously over so Charlie led her back to Adam. Once they approached Adam's group, he left her abruptly and headed for Sally and Betty Nelsen.

Adam was frowning. "You have a good time?"

"You're jealous."

"Of course I'm jealous," he growled. "I'll be working all summer and that bum will be hanging around you. I'll be gone next year and he'll be right there beside you."

"Oh, Adam," she wailed. "Don't spoil tonight. You don't have to be jealous of anyone, ever."

She reached up and touched his arm, saying, "Dance with me."

Adam smiled and took her hand. He said, "As soon as the music starts playing again."

She laughed as she realized that the music had stopped. Now she said, "When you leave this fall, I'll date lots of fellows, not just one. That's a promise."

"How about Charlie?"

"Maybe Charlie will be one of them, I'm not sure. But you and I have something special. And I'll have myself, too."

The music started again and Adam reached for her hand, leading her out to the dance floor. At that moment, Michelle thought, *I'll never be happier than this*. For Michelle, the crepe paper streamers were silken threads of love. The band, which earlier had seemed only adequate, was now playing enchanted music.

The future would take care of itself. She and Adam were together now and she was on her way to being her own person, too.

WILDFIRE.

Move from one breathtaking romance to another with the #1 Teen Romance line in the country!

NEW WILDFIRES! $1.95 each

- ☐ MU32539-6   **BLIND DATE** Priscilla Maynard
- ☐ MU32541-8   **NO BOYS?** McClure Jones
- ☐ MU32538-8   **SPRING LOVE** Jennifer Sarasin
- ☐ MU31930-2   **THAT OTHER GIRL** Conrad Nowels

BEST-SELLING WILDFIRES! $1.95 each

- ☐ MU31981-7   **NANCY AND NICK** Caroline B. Cooney
- ☐ MU32513-X   **SECOND BEST** Helen Cavanagh
- ☐ MU31849-7   **YOURS TRULY, LOVE, JANIE** Ann Reit
- ☐ MU31566-8   **DREAMS CAN COME TRUE** Jane Claypool Miner
- ☐ MU32369-3   **HOMECOMING QUEEN** Winifred Madison
- ☐ MU31261-8   **I'M CHRISTY** Maud Johnson
- ☐ MU30324-4   **I'VE GOT A CRUSH ON YOU** Carol Stanley
- ☐ MU32361-X   **THE SEARCHING HEART** Barbara Steiner
- ☐ MU31710-5   **TOO YOUNG TO KNOW** Elisabeth Ogilvie
- ☐ MU32430-6   **WRITE EVERY DAY** Janet Quin-Harkin
- ☐ MU30956-0   **THE BEST OF FRIENDS** Jill Ross Klevin

Scholastic Inc.,
P.O. Box 7502, 2932 E. McCarty Street, Jefferson City, MO 65102

Please send me the books I have checked above. I am enclosing $_____ (please add $1.00 to cover shipping and handling). Send check or money order— no cash or C.O.D.'s please.

Name_____

Address_____

City_____State/Zip_____

Please allow four to six weeks for delivery.   9/83